The Cycle

The Riven Trilogy

Book 2

A.R. Knight

Chapter 1

Family Dynamics

Selena hacked the dead man with her cleaver. The spirit was young, cloaked in hospital rags, and vicious. Blue flames poured from the edges of Selena's weapon and curled around the spirit's snarling body. His eyes glazed over into blank nothing.

My lash whipped forward and snagged the outstretched arm of another spirit reaching for Selena's neck. Gnarled hands betraying the spirit's own mind, her perception of herself as she crossed to Riven an old woman. Also wearing a hospital gown. As were all the spirits in the courtyard, near the large palace where

Alec and I had fought a ghoul not too many nights ago.

"Behind," I said, and Selena whirled, going low with her cleaver while I held the spirit back. Selena made contact and the spirit howled her rage before the pale fire burned it away.

"You can't forget that," I said. "Your back is always vulnerable."

"Not when you're around," Selena said, giving me a quick smile. Not much time for talking. More spirits climbed out of the breach, a glowing pit on the flagstones in front of us that, like a pond reflecting the sky, showed a hospital ward on the other side.

A containment unit housing so many dying from the disease. They called it the flu, and it was wrecking the world. It would wreck this one too if we didn't close the breaches fast enough. To my right, a pair of spirits worked together to annihilate their brethren.

Graham, looking like an out-sized carnival barker and sporting a spiked hammer, swept raging spirits aside with long swings. That gave space for Katherine to work, her hooked batons carving up and propelling her from one spirit to the next, wrapping each one in blue flame as she moved.

"It's almost ready," Anna said from my left. She held a tablet with a blue sapphire in the middle. A device centuries older than I was, a product of unknown creation that had been passed from guide to guide and now found itself in the hands of a former sneak.

"On it," I said, grabbing my large crossbow from its holster on my back. With Selena providing cover, I clicked the lever on the left side of the stock to load up bolts tinged with blue, and then turned the right crank. Slotted one, aimed, and shot a spirit just as it turned toward us, its eyes awash with the same blue glow as our calming fire. The bolt hit the spirit in the chest and fire burst out, matching its eyes. But when the fire finished crawling over its body, the spirit's eyes were plain, blank. Ready for the Cycle.

Fired again, and a third time. Each bolt wrangled a spirit with blue fire. Each one bought us a bit of time. Brought us one step closer.

"It's ready," Anna said. "I'm going for it."

I pushed the lever on the crossbow, switching to the normal, hard-hitting metal bolts. I tracked Anna as she ran towards the center of the glowing breach and fired at any spirits that came close. Each bolt slammed into and shoved away a pair of outstretched hands, wild and crazy eyes, and gnashing teeth.

"Back up!" I yelled to Graham and Katherine. Selena caught the words too, ran behind me, and kept going. They had to get out of range.

Anna reached the center of the breach and pressed in on the sapphire. It sank into the tablet, slick blue lines shooting out in all directions, tendrils reaching for the edges of the glowing portal. They lanced through any spirits, enveloping them in that same blue glow. The raging ones in hospital rags turned to simple bodies, standing there without a thought left in their heads. Other tendrils grabbed the edges and pulled them closed, shrinking the portal against the flagstones until, seconds later, there was nothing more than the hard gray rock of the courtyard beneath our feet. Another breach closed.

"It gets easier every time," Selena said as she walked back to my side.

"These spirits were sick," I replied. "Patients that weren't strong. Some breaches are harder than others."

"Oh come on," Selena said. "Can you at least say I did a good job?"

"You're getting better. Still have to watch your back. If I wasn't there, you'd have been caught."

"Who cares?" Selena said. "I'm already dead."

I shook my head. Didn't have a good come back for that one. Just because Selena was a spirit and couldn't actually die again, didn't mean she couldn't get hurt. Didn't mean she couldn't wind up broken and weak and waiting to recover. "Even if that's true, I bet Nicholas wouldn't like repairing all your stuff."

"He lives for it," Selena said.

That cockiness. That was a new one. An unexpected bonus of bringing Selena into the more dangerous parts of this life. She'd wanted to add adventure to her endless days in Riven and had taken to it like a rat to a sewer. I couldn't suppress a laugh.

"Is that enough for your quota?" Graham asked. "Or has Piotr increased the number again?"

"Still at one breach." Which was a ludicrous amount. We'd never had an expectation to close a breach on every night in Riven before. Normally, it was a set number of spirits. Three, four, maybe even five that we had to find and reduce to walking mannequins heading for the Cycle. That far-off place where Riven cleansed the dead.

"It's not getting any better," Katherine said, panning a slow look around the courtyard. "Every time we're wandering around, there are more. And more guides to go with them."

"Piotr's been recruiting," I said. "There's no telling when the war is going to end. We're taking everybody we can get."

"Except for some people." Anna handed me the tablet and I slotted it back in my belt.

"I'm working on it," I said. "Sneaks don't do themselves any favors."

"Not everybody can afford to be noble and righteous all the time. Some of us need to get paid to survive."

"The guides were always too stuffy," Graham said. "All pomp. All bravado."

"Quit it," Katherine said. "You loved them just as much as I did. Besides, without being a guide, you wouldn't have met me."

"And then I wouldn't exist," I said. "Come on, let's get back to the apartment. It's almost time to cross back."

Chapter 2

New Toys, Old Questions

In the few months since we'd freed Graham, there had been one objective for the apartment: to expand. The usual routine was to clear a breach and hit my quota, and then come back to this place and clean the next floor down. Put in new doors.

Scavenge materials and work with Nicholas to prep the new living space.

The nutty scientist now had the ground-floor lab that he wanted. As we came back, Nicholas was audible from a block away, buzzing around with his machines. How the man managed to craft working ovens, generators, and other miracles from Riven's desolate ruins stunned me. But then, that's why I bound him in the first place.

The second and third floors belonged to Graham and Katherine, with Selena taking the top for herself. The tall and thin building now resembled an actual residence. We made furniture, stripped what cloth we could find in other places to put together bedsheets and even some semblance of carpet. The whole thing an exercise to make the spirits feel more like the humans they once were.

"Do you like it?" Nicholas asked as we walked in. He gestured to a far wall on which he'd carved a map of the city. Hooks, little spikes, were driven in nearly every inch. On some of those hooks hung glowing blue dots. "Each one is a breach. The stones work like your resonators. The breaches pulse a certain signature. A wavelength that I can catch with these little gadgets."

The scientist held up what looked like a pair of beads fused together with a wire running around them. Next to the map Nicholas kept a bent metal barrel full of the things, with a thick lid on top. Nicholas led us over to it, continuing his explanation. "I leave one out, and when it picks up a signal, because every single breach is slightly different, the wire vibrates and the beads glow blue. Then I measure the frequency to determine the distance, and that tells me roughly where it is." One of the dots on the map faded. "And that tells me when a breach has been sealed. Genius, right?"

"You never cease to amaze," I said.

"So does this tell us where we should be going?" Anna asked. "Or where other guides are more likely to be?"

Nicholas stared at her for a moment. Then hummed, tapping his lips. "I suppose I haven't thought of that. Perhaps that's the next thing. Find a way to track where the guides are going."

"Now if you could do that," I said, "then you and the others would be safe."

"The guides would be safe, you mean," Graham said. The spirit wasn't wrong. That spiked hammer of his could probably take care of most of the guides we had. With Katherine beside him, I would pity any poor guide that tried to wrangle them.

"All the same," Katherine said. "It's best if we avoid each other."

"I love it, Nicholas," Anna said and the scientist beamed at her. "Keep going. And, speaking of guides, it's time for me to check out."

"Anna," I said. "Come by Ezra's in the morning. I've got something for you."

Anna nodded. Her exit prompted the rest of us to make our own. I went with Selena to the fourth floor, the top. I thought it funny how we'd filled the apartment with furniture. Things absolutely meaningless to a spirit in Riven. Selena didn't need to sleep. She didn't need to eat. She never, barring injury, became tired. No day to shade and night to light in the perpetually gray monotone of this world.

When you walked into her place, it looked, it felt, like a home in a world that needed none.

"You're bringing her to Ezra's?" Selena said as soon as we shut the door behind us.

"She doesn't know yet," I said, "but Piotr approved the application. She's going to be inducted as a guide."

"She already is, more or less, right?"

"If guides caught her in Riven with a weapon that could wrangle, they'd probably try to blind her."

"Sometimes I wonder if that would be so bad," Selena said. "Never having to come back to this place again?"

I followed Selena through the living room, back to normal after Nicholas moved down below. Selena covered the walls with her black and white drawings, mostly cityscapes that Selena could see out from the balcony. Where we went now.

Off in the distance, over the gray tops of buildings, the occasional shower of colored sparks flew through the air. Guides communicating their positions to one another. Riven looked the same as it always did. Full of buildings with no real architectural pattern. Some bearing the pointed, targeted stone of centuries ago while others had the sheer walls and multistory design of more modern cities. Though no one could recall ever seeing a building come up in Riven, the variety made it hard for me to accept that it had all been created at once. One certainty, though; Riven was falling apart.

Walking the streets was a tour through disaster. Some buildings crumbling in their entirety, others only in pieces. A floor collapsed here, a wall knocked over there. The decay continued to spread through Riven. Partly due to the fighting; the endless waves of angry spirits trashing things in their fury until a guide put them to rest. Partly due to the mysterious, gradual decline of this place. A dying world.

I glanced up at the gray sky, a permanent mist blunting the white light above. Ash flakes filtered down around us; a constant presence floating along on a breeze that came from nowhere. Like snow that never melted, that wasn't cold.

"It's a gift," I said. "Everyone else has to sleep. Has to dream. I get to spend these hours here with you."

"You're such a sap sometimes, Carver," Selena said, but I caught her smile. "It's much better now than it used to be. Thanks for taking me along."

"You're getting good with that thing," I nodded to the cleaver locked into a holster on her belt. The jackets we wore, long trench coats that provided protection, weren't always the easiest to fight in. They were heavy. The long sleeves and flapping cloth could get in the way. But Selena learned fast and she came on all of our raids.

I wasn't sure if my girlfriend being a murderous expert with a cleaver was comforting or not, but it fit that she'd learned to use the weapon that killed her.

"I want to go with you," Selena said. "When you go after him."

"We don't even know where he is. Who he is," I said. "I've only heard him called 'the Master'."

"We found your mother," Selena said. "We can find him too."

"So long as he doesn't find us first," I said.

"If he does, we'll be ready," Selena replied with all the confidence of one who couldn't die.

Chapter 3

Guide
About Town

I jerked awake in Chicago. I would fall asleep in my bed in Riven's clock tower, the base from which our Chicago guides operated, and wake up in a world full of color. With whirring machines and, outside the window, swarms of drifting zeppelins. The war burned abroad, and Chicago's industries changed to suit the country's needs.

I glanced over at the growing pile of mail underneath my vacuum tube. A funnel that sucked letters up from the street and shot them into my apartment. The latest paper sat on top. Above the fold ran a piece by my most-

and least-liked reporter, a guy by the name of Opperman.

"Death by disease, or war?" the headline ran. I skimmed the article, wincing at the endless hyperbole Opperman employed. Every battle a glorious victory or horrendous defeat. Every death multiplied to the thousandth in its cost to humanity. Every outbreak of sniffles the next doom to sweep the land.

I used to laugh at pieces like these. The ridiculous notion that I lived in the world described by these pages. Not anymore. The articles weren't all embellishment. They weren't proved false by the facts at play. Opperman had finally found a world that suited him. One that brought more disaster every day.

I slipped on my mask, a black and gold number that hid my face, that combined with my coat to announce to the world what I was. A guide. A special kind of creature, worthy of both respect and fear. Living proof of a place nobody wanted to know.

Which give me plenty of room on the crowded streets, and even earned me a mechanical nod of deference from a passing pilot in his mech. The giant two-legged things, twenty feet tall, were everywhere these days. Their twin smokestacks looming above the metal barrels of their guns, belching hot black into the air. Stomping around and making sure their dire threat brought peace to the streets.

As times went, there had been better.

Crowds filled the train downtown, as ever. Life churned on, and so the throngs of businessmen, scientists, and everyone that supported them continued making their treks to their respective parts of the city. Suits to soot-stained coats to mechanics in greasy overalls—all the classes came together in common movement.

I always had my own seat. My own space. At first I'd been troubled by the fear that came over everyone's eyes when they saw me, that nervous look that shaded their glances. A reminder of a nightmare they never wanted to believe. Now I enjoyed stretching my legs.

Ezra's defined *classic*. A fixture that made itself known to anyone passing by. The gold letters on the outside, and that deep crimson veneer that said a trip into this bar had the potential to change your life. At least for a drink or two.

For me, at 8:30 in the morning, coffee would be that drink. I slipped inside the door and stood for a minute in the purification area. Dirty air, that musty grime of Chicago's, filtered out as purified sweet stuff came in. I pulled off the mask, its respirator no longer necessary, and went inside my favorite place in the city.

"You are here. I was beginning to have my doubts," Alec said to me as I walked in. He sat at our usual table, a circle big enough to sit six, though the two of us were often its only occupants, now that my mentor, friend, and former leader Bryce had slipped away to a quiet life with his family. Alec already had a pot of coffee sitting there, this time with three mugs instead of two.

"I don't think Anna is used to getting up early," I said. "I'm usually the first to cross back by a long shot."

"One of many changes she will need to be making," Alec said. "Anna cannot be both sneak *and* guide."

"Once we start paying her, she'll be able to afford to leave that life behind."

We spent the wait swapping stories. I told Alec about closing the breach last night; our team of five wiping through spirits and sending them to the Cycle. Alec did what he usually preferred, running around alone, picking off angry spirits when they didn't see him coming. Of course, our current quota made that harder. It would be suicide to try and close a breach by yourself.

"I join up," Alec said. "It hurts, but I need to make friends anyway. Find a different group every night, help them close a breach, and then I go do what I want."

"Look at you," I said. "A team player. Never thought I'd see the day."

"These days are full of surprises," Alec said, nodding back to the door.

Anna stood there, in her usual working woman's attire, looking lost. Of any place in Chicago to go, a sneak would find Ezra's the least accommodating. It'd been a guide meeting place for centuries. And sneaks, people that were able to cross into Riven and did so without approval or training from the guides, were definitely not welcome.

"Anna," I said. "We're over here."

She flashed a grateful smile, and took a seat. I slid across a mug full of coffee to her and she stared at it, then looked up. "I'm more of a tea person."

"Oh, the first error already," Alec said. "Carver, I think we made a mistake."

"We can't all be perfect," I said. "She'll just have to work harder to make up for it."

"Sorry," Anna said. "I thought I heard you needed more guides? I don't think now is the time to get picky."

"Truth," I said. "Which brings us to why you're here."

I nodded to the bartender, and the gentleman brought out, from behind the bar, a crate and carried it to the table. From his waist, bartender took out a small device, an opener, and slotted it into the lock in the center top of the crate. The bartender turned his wrist and moved the opener in a circle, winding the gears on the crate and eventually popping the thing open, its flaps falling to the side and revealing the contents.

A new mask, white and silver and looking like curled smoke. A card with her name. Beneath both of those, an official coat. Long and thick, and emblazoned with the circle and bars that declared its wearer a guide.

"Does this mean what I think it means?" Anna asked.

"Over my strenuous objections," Alec said, disarming the comment with a wink.

"We'd like to make you an official guide," I said. "If you accept."

"Is there any doubt?" Anna replied. "Why wouldn't I?"

"You have to give it up," I said. "You can't do both. A sneak can't be a guide."

Anna passed her eyes between Alec and I, thinking. Then she nodded. "Riven is getting too dangerous for sneaks anyway. If I can help make it safer, then it would be the right thing to do."

"She's a noble one," Alec said. "This is the worst idea."

"Be quiet, Alec," I said. "Welcome to the guides, Anna. We're happy to have you."

"If we're going to have to take her on," Alec said. "Then the only way I accept is if we celebrate." He looked at Anna's full coffee cup. "Please tell me you're okay with beer?"

"Now that I enjoy," Anna said, and Alec gave an exaggerated sigh of relief.

Chapter 4

Strange Ride

I'd be the first to say that I like a good drink. Or several. Being a guide came with the most wonderful way to avoid a hangover: cross to Riven and the headaches went away. Hunt spirits for a few hours, and when I crossed back I'd be feeling fine. So that evening, on the train back to my apartment, ginned up from all the, well, gin, I looked forward to crossing over, finding Selena, and maybe a breach or two to put to rest.

I had my own pair of seats on this route, a double facing me wide open even as other people stood in the center of the aisle. Nobody wanted to look at me in my mask. Nobody wanted to get on the wrong side of someone they might run into after they've died, someone who made souls cease to exist. So I wasn't expecting anybody to bother me. So when a man sat down across from me, and maybe the alcohol helped, it took me a minute to notice.

He didn't say anything, just stared at me and out the window at the passing cityscape. I gave him the once-over. He wore a cheap mask, not carved metal like my own, but one made of cloth and rough edges. No style. The could be said for the rest of his clothes. A workman's vest and a ratty jacket, trousers stained and worn. I couldn't quite make out his eyes beneath that mask, but the man's slouch suggested they would be tired.

"Funny how no one likes to sit across from a guide," the man said by way of a greeting.

Took me a second to compose a reply. I'd settled into the silent stupor that so often takes travelers on trains, rising back to consciousness only when their stop is called. "I don't mind."

"It's like being afraid of your destiny," the man said. His words, the leaden tones in his voice, shook me out of my boozy haze. People didn't usually say lines like that, much less to someone they didn't know. Even less to a guide.

"I suppose you could say that," I said. "But not everyone needs a guide to get where they're going."

"Especially not one like you," the man said.

I straightened up. "What was that, again?"

"Carver Reed," the man said. "I've been trying to find you. Riding these trains back and forth most days for the last week."

If I'd been sleepily sobering up before, I woke up now. I'd been hunted before, in Riven, by the kind of spirits you don't want to go up against. Here in Chicago, in the real world, people didn't know my name. Not unless they were a guide, or I knew them personally. I didn't advertise.

"Now," the man continued, "I see you're getting a little bit nervous. I'll contend that you ought not to be. And also contend that you ought to stay seated."

The man shifted his jacket enough so that I saw, hanging from a shoulder holster, the dull bronze of a pistol. When the man saw that I'd noticed, he closed the jacket again, but left his right hand on the weapon.

"Is this how you always make friends?" I asked.

"Only the ones I want to keep," the man said. "I feel like it's only fair, as I know yours, that you know mine. Inman."

He extended his left hand across the gap between our seats. I wanted to spit on it. Or slap it away. But I wasn't armed. My weapons lived on the other side. So I gripped his hand with mine and we shook in a single pump.

"Well, Inman, you've come onto my train. You've made a subtle threat. You going to explain why?"

"I will," Inman said. "But before I do, we're going to get off this train."

We were not at my stop. In fact, we were coming up on a switch point. A station where, if you wanted, you could jump to trains heading farther west, out of the city and into the country. The station itself was a snarl of stairs and platforms, trains running in and out in a constant blare of whistles. Chaos or perfect efficiency depending on your perspective.

Inman gestured for me to get up as the train slowed to a stop, and I didn't argue. Survival took priority, so I followed orders. I didn't really want to get shot, or start a fight with the guy on the train. Also, I had questions. What did he want, and why go about it this way?

We crossed the switch point, walking along an overpass above various tracks rattling as trains crossed beneath us. The smoke billowed around the glass enclosing the overpass, so it looked as if we were shrouded in momentary fog. We went passed the city routes, a couple heading north and the one heading south. Stopped at the thick rail going west.

"Gun or no," I said "I'm not going to leave the city."

"You will," Inman said. "But we're not going far. Only to the river."

"The river?"

Inman shook his head. "I forget how little you city folks know about your country. The Mississippi."

I knew the Mississippi. Of course I did. It didn't come to mind right away because I never left Chicago. Never needed to, and being a guide meant staying put. Crossing at a new place brought risks. Never knew where in Riven you might wind up.

"Are we going fishing?" I asked.

"If you want to call it that. We're aiming to catch something a little different. You're the bait."

"That doesn't exactly make me want to go with you."

"What if I told you that the man we're trying to catch is the one that bound your father. That tried to have you killed. That murdered your mother?" Inman replied.

The Master. They were after him too. And they had a plan, or at least it sounded like it. I must not have reacted fast enough, because Inman kept going.

"Now we know it's not your fault," Inman continued. "You were just born, but sometimes existing has a way of forcing people's hands. I've lost too many friends to that man, and I don't even know his name. With you, I think he's desperate. Sees you as his only chance. Which gives us an opportunity."

Two hours of slight conversation later, the train pulled into the station, doors sliding open in front of us. This time, when Inman waved me forward, I didn't hesitate. If they wanted to catch the Master, if they wanted to kill the man that had brought my family so much pain, I'd be their bait.

Chapter 5
The Wild Woods

Nobody wore a mask. After years in Chicago's packed pollution, I noticed that first. The people pouring off the train around us, greeting friends and relatives, all had their faces out in the evening sunlight. When I breathed, the air had a different flavor. Not the sweet sterile taste of Ezra's and other purifiers, but instead heavy with nature. The sense and textures of wildflowers and pine needles, the burning smoke of fires not for forging industry but for cooking food.

Around the station, as far as I could see, stretched arcing tree-covered bluffs racing alongside the endless churn of the Mississippi

River. The town we'd stopped in nestled amongst the limestone cliffs, curling back away from the river and up into the hills.

Inman pointed down the road, a gravelly affair crowded with animals. Horses. A couple of small jalopies, but otherwise the neighing creatures were the order of the day. You didn't see those on Chicago's streets. Nobody wanted to clean up after them, so once you hit the city limits, you stabled your horse and rode the trains like everybody else. Or you walked.

Inman led me to a trio of horses, all brown, and all, Inman explained, the gentlest of mares. Another man sat on the third horse, wearing a guide's coat and looking at me as though I were some kind of a traitor. The man's glare matched his angry beard, a gnarled mass of black and gray that seemed to be taking over his face. A stained charcoal hat sat on his head, the wide brim casting shade across his eyes so that their green appeared to glow in the setting sun.

"I see you found him," the man said. "You know how to ride?"

"Not a clue," I said. "Not much use for it in the city. Or in Riven."

"Then today, you learn," the man replied. "Climb into the saddle, hold on to that little knob in front of you, and I'll lead her."

"It's not too far," Inman said.

I watched Inman climb into his saddle, then tried to copy the move. Stuck my right foot in the stirrup and then swung my left leg over. It would've worked, I'm sure, if I'd had a looser coat. Something that didn't get snagged on the end of the saddle. I wound up flopping my way over and wriggling around with my chest pressed to the horse before finally getting myself arranged.

When I sat up, I saw Inman repressing a chuckle and the other guy shaking his head. The crowd joined in. Claps and whistles. Nothing like a little humiliation to keep your ego in check.

"This is Mead," Inman said as we started moving along. "You might've noticed he was a guide."

I bounced around on the horse, trying to adjust to the constant motion. I slid back and forth in the saddle and tried to keep hold of the knob in front of me, alternating between that and a death-grip on the horse's hair. For her part, the mare didn't seem to give a crap about whatever I did. She followed Mead and his guiding hand on the rope tied around her bridle without complaint.

"I might have," I said when it felt safe to talk, to take a bit of my attention away from staying in the saddle.

"You might've noticed that he doesn't much care for you," Inman said.

"I might've."

"Mostly because you buried his friend beneath a tower of rubble," Inman said. "Which is how we know about you at all."

"Barth?"

That spirit had been another one working for the Master. Barth had performed murderous experiments in hopes of finding a way out of Riven. He'd murdered guides in his tower, and with each failure, enslaved the subject to join his bound spirit army. All in the hopes of finding a way back to life he once had.

Then Barth picked the wrong fight with Alec, Bryce and I. Tried to bring his own tower down on top of us and wound up caught in it.

"That's the one," Inman said. "We'd been preparing our own move on the tower. We wanted to try to free him. Send him to the Cycle. Then you took care of it for us."

"Sounds like I did you a favor."

We turned up out of the town onto a winding trail to the bluffs. The narrow pathway curled beneath leafy trees, adding the sound of songbirds to the crunch of hooves on dirt and rock.

"I think Barth deserved what he got," Inman said. "But some of us thought he could be saved. Some of us thought that if we'd been able to get him back, Barth would've told us where to find the Master. Now all we've got is you."

"How did you even find me?" I asked. "I didn't see anyone there after the tower fell."

"Spirits talk plenty once you bind them," Mead grumbled up front.

"We found some of Barth's old spirits standing around the remnants of his tower," Inman replied. "So now you understand. You owe Mead, really. It was his right to be the one to help his friend."

His right. Sure. Barth had been doing his experiments for years by the time we took care of him. Mead hadn't been in a hurry. But I didn't bother saying that. Bryce had pressed a cautionary attitude into me, despite my attempts to ignore it. In Riven, caution meant being calm around spirits that hadn't already turned. Keeping a spirit from getting agitated meant saving your own life. I wanted to keep Mead from deciding I'd make a better bait with a few cathartic bruises.

Inman didn't talk for a while after that. Perhaps the glowing embers of the sun setting behind the bluffs, filtering its purple orange rays through the branches of the trees mesmerized him as it did me. The flickering wings of bats replaced the birds, their chirps and chimes swapped with buzzing bugs. I sat in silence. Experienced it.

Didn't have this in Chicago.

Eventually we came into a campground; a series of tents and ramshackle cabins set up around a large fire pit. Another ten to fifteen men and women worked around it, cooking food and cleaning, doing laundry in a washing well set up nearby. I felt like I'd fallen down a hole and come out several centuries ago.

"What's the point?" I said as Inman helped me off the horse. "Living way out here, you can't be on our calls. Can't be connected."

"We're not guides anymore," Inman said. "We don't have any need to pay attention to what you're all doing."

"Why?"

"Eventually you get sick of following orders. Especially when you're told to forget your friends."

Inman pointed me towards one of the cabins and I, ignoring my growling stomach, went. People turned to glance at me, but most didn't stop their work. Disciplined. In the cabin were pair of cots, if you could call them that. More like bedrolls with blankets on top. Inman gestured to the one on the right.

"Go ahead. Lay down and cross over," Inman said.

"No dinner?"

"You'll get plenty to eat if we make it through this."

"You know, if I cross here, I won't have anything," I said. "No weapons, nothing to help."

"You're the bait," Inman said. "The bait's not supposed to help."

I thought about protesting, but Inman pulled out that pistol of his, held it at his waist. No choice but to cross. Which I didn't mind. In spite of everything, I wanted to meet the Master. Even if it killed me.

Chapter 6

The Bait

Normally Riven presented the same scene when I crossed over: a stonework room with a line of beds beside me, a rack of weapons in front, and a stone table and chairs for waiting until my friends joined.

Here, I crossed over onto a pile of grass. Not the summer kind; the wavy green and soft stuff of childhood dreams. These stalks were crinkly and white. Like walking on dried straw. Or a scrub brush. Trees rose up around me, blocking Riven's gray light, their spindly branches sprouting black leaves in all directions. I had my coat, my mask and nothing else. The things

I carried on my person crossed over with me. No lash, no knife, no defenses.

Felt a hand grab my arm and pull me along. I turned and saw Mead's set face, the glower beneath the man's scraggly beard.

"It's this way," Mead said.

"Didn't you quit the guides because you didn't like their orders? And yet, here you are ordering me around?"

"This is more important than your sarcasm," Mead said, but at least he dropped my arm and let me walk behind him. Unlike the trail through the bluffs leading to the campground, the forest in Riven had no scent. Nothing other than the usual bland blankness of Riven air. I breathed it in, even though I didn't have to. One of the first things they taught a new guide, told you when you cross over to hold your breath as long as you could. Then you found you could do it forever.

We reached a gap in the woods, one that Mead and the others had made. Trees had been cleared, their stumps ringless and solid gray. One by one the former guides showed up and formed a ring around me, pushing me towards the center. Inman came, gave me a nod.

"So is this a sacrifice, or what?" I asked him. "Because this doesn't seem like a trap to me."

"We don't know where he'll come from," Inman said. "But we know he'll try to get to you."

"How are you going to draw the Master to me? You want me to dance? Sing a song?"

Inman laughed, shook his head. "Carver, in another life, I imagine we would've had a few good times together."

Minutes later, the ring tight and everyone standing ready, their hands on their weapons, Mead brought two fingers to his lips and whistled. I couldn't see them, but I assumed there were other people that lit the fires. Raw flame, not the pale blue wrangling kind, shot up the trees around us.

I saw them now, the ragged sheets and paper and wood gathered from elsewhere tied up around the trees. The fires caught quickly and burned upwards, climbing the gray trunks and lashing into the black leaves. The sudden burst of color threw me, played with my eyes and a mind that expected nothing other than the endless gray. Real ash joined the omnipresent flakes as the fires engulfed the trees around the square.

"You think he'll see this?" I called to Inman.

"We know he's around here," Inman said. "Tracked him this far. But he keeps slipping. Which is why we need you."

I watched from the edges of the ring, the backs of all the heads of these guides waiting for their chance to exact vengeance for some wrong or another. I wished that I could've stood with them.

Especially when the screaming started.

Chapter 7

The Master

The shouts came from beyond the ring, in the flickering darkness outside the flame-lit clearing. I watched, but none of the guides shifted. Nobody displayed any signs of panic as the howling drew closer. The same wail I'd heard a thousand times. A wave of angry spirits pouring from a breach, ones pulled together to form a mob of horrors. Left unchecked, the source of the howls, that screeching rage, might form a ghoul.

One of the guides raised her hand, pointing with her hatchet. I looked that way and saw, at the edge of the courtyard, a figure. A tall, thick, cloaked person. In the firelight, the man's black robes shimmered, laced with gold filament. His face hidden by a ridged, obsidian mask, as though forged from volcanic rock. In both hands, down at his waist, he held a long, wide blade that went half his height and perhaps more.

As the ring around me turned their attention to him, the man raised the blade and jammed its point into the ground. As soon as the edge made contact with Riven's earth, if it could be called that, the screeching that surrounded us shifted, like a siren in the distance suddenly turning towards me.

The spirits descended out of the dark.

The guides drew their weapons with their own cheers and battle cries. Most were names, some I recognized, of guides that had fallen over the years. Friends lost to this nightmare world. I watched as they met the crash of spirits head-on.

Only these weren't the scraggly rabble Selena and I had fought earlier, the sickly and desperate. The confused and lost. No. These spirits were bound, these were trained and hardened and though they came at the guides without more than stones and scraps for weapons, they moved with purpose and they moved together.

The spirits weren't in soldier's uniforms or the rags of the hospital-bound. Instead, they were uniformly different. As though coming from a dozen times and places. Some wore armor of an Eastern past, while others raged in little more than loin clothes and thin robes.

I watched a guide swing at one with a pair of long knives, blitzing slashes and weaves only to see the spirit backpedal out of reach and, after a near miss thrust, a second spirit dove from the dark at the guide, rending and tearing at his face.

On the other side, Inman and Mead worked together. The latter using a pair of short spears to stab and withdraw, sending one spirit after another away with blue fire. Inman complemented the man with a pair of pistols, weapons I hadn't seen much of in Riven. You never knew how many spirits might be around the next corner, and running out of ammunition meant running out of your life. But Inman's guns popped one after another, sending shots into the spirits and opening them up for Mead's wrangling stab.

I kept rotating, tried to keep my eyes everywhere at once. The ring still held, but its boundaries were getting loose. Spirits clawed closer and closer as guides fell or shifted out of the line. I tried to keep my eyes everywhere, minimize the chance that I could find myself attacked without defenses. I had to be ready to run.

A fist hit my shoulder and knocked me to the ground. I rolled with the impact and wound up on my back, pushing away from the towering figure standing above me. The Master himself, carving in through the ring.

"Carver Reed," the Master said, his voice a hollow baritone, like the low notes on an organ. "I'll be taking you now."

The Master held his blade in his left hand and reached for me with his right. I leaned forward and grabbed his wrist, pulling him, trying to trip him up. The Master braced himself and, instead, yanked me to my feet. Then he pointed outside the ring, to somewhere in the distance.

"Walk," the Master said, ignoring the continuing fight. He had good reason to. More spirits kept pouring out of the dark and the guides were overwhelmed. One after another fell to the tricks and traps of the Master's devious army.

"I'm really not feeling it," I said.

"You know what I want," the Master replied. "To open the gate, you're the only one that needs to die. If you don't walk, I'll make sure everyone you love dies as well."

I took threats as seriously as the person who made them. If I didn't think they could pull through, if I thought they're punching above their weight, then I'd laugh and move on. With the Master, I started walking.

"You're not taking him," Mead announced, diving at the Master with his spears stabbing. I watched the guide attack, his first strike heading straight for the Master's chest. The great sword sat too low, too far away to be brought up to block. So the Master twisted, allowed Mead to come ever so close to sticking the Master on the point of a spear. So close, but not close enough.

I heard a crack, the report of Inman's pistol, and the Master grunted. The large man brought his right hand up to his shoulder where I could see a tear in the coat.

"That's for Barth," Inman said. "This is for everyone else."

The guide raised his other pistol, aimed right at the Master's face, and fired. The bullet struck the mask. It hit that shimmering rock, and bounced off. Blew a chunk away, revealing a hint of skin in that shadowy light. A glint of teeth. And then the Master moved.

Mead turned from his strike and stabbed at the Master's back, a hair too slow. The Master ducked forward and charged at Inman. Mead's spear grazed the Master's coat, but missed the flesh. Inman worked his first pistol, slotting another bullet, raised it, and then the Master's sword swept up and carved the man in half like I would cut a slice of bread.

I wanted to yell, to do something, but my hands were empty and my throat had lost any voice it ever had. I could only think to run. I saw Mead's wild-eyed face as he leapt with spears flashing forward and the Master, in a smooth motion, swinging his great sword around to meet the attack, and then I turned away to the forest.

The gray dark beyond the burning trees had me stumbling over the brittle grass. My eyes recovering from the bright orange light. I tried to remember where I crossed over, where Mead first grabbed me.

If visible terrors filled Riven's dense city, its forest; dark, quiet and creeping, gave rise to more insidious fears. My mind conjured up grasping claws, raking arms, and the hideous faces of those old, enraged spirits. Every step brought me past another tree, under another branch where any hell might lurk.

Bryce had spent years drilling the fear from me. Forcing reaction from panic to poise, to treat the unusual with calculated tactics. Then, I'd had weapons. Friends. A chance for success. Here I ran alone from a merciless enemy with allies in the shadows.

And yet, my feet flew with purpose. I pushed away numb frenzy gripping my nerves and focused on the grass, on the rays of gray light slipping through that canopy. I found my path and pressed on.

I recalled the tree had been near, the depression in the grass that indicated guides had used the spot as a bed more than once. The screaming behind me grew softer, more sporadic as the remaining members of Inman's band shared his fate.

There. The flattened bed of grass, nestled in between the roots of that large damned tree.

I dove onto the grass, turned over, and closed my eyes. Shut away the dead.

Chapter 8

Leftovers

When I crossed into Riven, the camp had been bustling with activity. When I crossed back in the dead of night, only the insects and the far-off cries of a loon gave me company. I didn't move. Not for a minute, anyway. A body lied in the bed to my right. I could see it through the scattered bits of moonlight bleeding through the cabins loosely thatched ceiling.

I recognized the face. The coat. The bronzed pistol on the ground next to the limp hand. No breath came from those lips, no rising and falling chest to denote the living human body. Inman had died in Riven, and so he died here as well. Whatever that had been, whatever their thought to ambush the Master had been based on, it hadn't accounted for the numbers. They hadn't known what they were going into, hadn't known what they were drawing out, only that they could.

I stood up and walked from the cabin and around the campsite. Bodies were scattered on bedrolls, in the other small cabins, around the dying embers of small fires. Not a single one still alive. All of these guides, these former guides, had given themselves to a doomed mission.

I wanted to despair right then. They didn't need to die. All of these guides could've helped with the breaches, could have helped keep Riven alive. Instead they been hacked to pieces going after one person. One soul. A waste.

But they had known where to find him. The Master. Now I had a clue; the forest. West of Riven's city, and large. Only, their clearing could've been anywhere beneath its dark leaves. So I searched the campground for anything that might give me a location. A place to travel to so I could find the Master again.

Anything that might help me avenge my brothers and sisters.

I knew that if I hadn't been on that train, that if Inman hadn't found me, then tonight wouldn't have happened. All these people would still be here. Or if we'd found the Master sooner. If Graham, Katherine, Alec and I had downed that monster, then these people would still be alive.

Selena would be shaking her head at me right now. I could hear her voice, telling me that I couldn't take responsibility for other people's actions. That everyone is who they want to be. That Mead and Inman and the rest of the guides knew what they were doing, and accepted whatever fate their actions would bring them.

Dwelling on death wasn't a luxury of our lives.

I found the map in the last cabin, pinned to the wall above Mead's motionless body. His spears hadn't struck home, apparently. Or if they had, the Master had taken Mead down with him. With nobody else in the camp moving, I didn't think it likely.

In the silver wisps of light, Mead's beard and emerald eyes, which had propped themselves wide open in the hideous state of the dead, struck me with a strange fear. A wild man meeting his wild fate. Would I, too, one day look like that? Alone and frozen in perpetual struggle against an unseen end?

I shook my head. Stay in the present, Carver. You're not dead yet. I tore my eyes from Mead's visage to the wall above him. The drawing.

Like Anna's maps in her hideout beneath the construction site in Chicago, the large sheet of paper held a crude drawing of Riven's city coupled with a more intricate mapping of the forest. Lines indicated routes that had been walked, pathways from a circle I assumed to be the clearing and whether or not, marked with red Xs, they'd encountered hostile forces. Words next to each of the Xs denoted the number of spirits found, whether those spirits, if captured, mentioned the Master. Towards the upper left part of the map the forest cut off into a swooping line. Two words written explained the shape.

The Mountain.

Below those words, on the edge of the line, written in jagged handwriting: *He lives here.*

The map fell off the wall when I pulled on it, rolled it up and shoved it into my coat pocket. Went back to the cabin with Inman's body, and took the pistol. Robbing the dead might seem disrespectful, but good weapons were valuable. I had a feeling Inman would rather see it used than lying there moldering away on the bluff. Patted down his pockets and found a smattering of bullets. Inman had left his pistol loaded, too. If he'd had to shoot me, Inman had been ready.

I went over to the horses, the whole group of them in various states of sleep and nervous wakefulness as I approached. The thought of trying to ride one back to the train station in the dark almost made me laugh. Almost broke the mood. Instead I opened the gate to their pen and walked away. Who knew when, if, anyone would come here. No reason to sentence the horses to a starving prisoner's fate.

Eerie shadows and illusions drifted along with me on my walk back to the town. I kept drifting into recollection, playing back the fight, and then the snap of a twig or an animal's surprised cry would jerk me back to the present. The short crossing to Riven and back didn't help—my muscles ached, my head eyes and throat dry and itching, my bones bleached and weary from the stress and the climb to the campsite.

So I held to the one positive. The one thing that made all of this misery worth it. I knew where to find him. The Master wouldn't be hiding much longer.

Chapter 9

Not Good News

I made it to the station by dawn and bought a ticket for the first train back to Chicago. Grabbed a newspaper and a stiff coffee for the ride and stood on the platform with a ragged band of commuters. They and I shared that quiet bond of a common destination, communicated by avoiding each other's eyes and keeping any words to absolute necessities.

The train roared in from the west, a great, hulking mass of steel and burning coal. Black smoke pitched out through a series of thick stacks. Whistles announced the boarding time and spindly metal gates shunted aside to let us climb on. Again I found myself left alone, my own corner of a car isolated as passengers clustered elsewhere.

I unfolded the paper, my companion for the ride, and I fell into its conversation. Yesterday, Opperman had the prime headline and today his bold name plastered across the paper's front again.

We'd joined the war in Europe. Whole bands of zeppelins crashing into each other above men and mechs blasting away in the trenches. Gas bombs flung back and forth, sending soldiers into delirious and deadly spirals. Ground wasn't being gained, but lives were being ground. Calls for sign-ups were increasing. The last peace talks had scattered to ashes amid the latest casualty reports. Desperate nations had scheduled the next attempt to start in a week, in New York, but Opperman gave a peaceful resolution low odds.

Humanity seemed resigned to burn itself to ashes.

Compounding the fighting were continued, frightening notices of contagion. Sickness spreading through America's major cities, sweeping from one borough to the next. The disease had come from overseas and, like the war, seemed intent on ruining everything it touched.

Masks were said to be effective, and avoiding the sick. I heard it there on the train. A cough, two rows ahead. A woman with a child.

And another; across the aisle from me. An older man staring out the window with a handkerchief pressed to his face. Even though we were miles yet from the city, the air still tasting clear, I pulled out my mask and slipped it on. Made sure the respirator worked.

Sometimes I had to remember that this world could kill me just as easily as Riven.

Still, even if the countries pulled themselves together, even if the scientists made a miracle cure to keep us all from falling victim to disease, none of it would matter if the breaches kept forming in Riven. None of it would matter if the dead clawed back into our world. None of it would matter if we couldn't find the Master and stop him.

I looked down at my coffee, the steam rising from the tall cup, I wanted a drink. And not this kind.

Chapter 10

A Long
Walk West

"The Mountain?" Graham said when I told him about the map. "That's not close."

We were back at the apartment, the whole group of us. I'd insisted. Only Alec, disappeared off on some rogue hunt, didn't show. So far the response had been skeptical. Even when I talked about Inman, Mead, and their sacrifice.

"We've tried to go there before," Katherine said. "When Graham and I were still alive."

Katherine paused for a second, I could see her struggling with the word. The idea. I'd never been a spirit, but I imagined part of it meant knowing all the time that you were no longer, well, you. Selena had talked about how she missed the tastes, the colors, and the sounds of the real world. She missed living.

"What I'm trying to say," Katherine continued. "Is that you can't make it there in one night. It takes days. You'll have to cross back before we get there."

"Then we'll try," I said. "I'll go as far as I can. At least to the border of the city. Once you get beyond that, there won't be other guides in your way."

"The forest doesn't need guides to be deadly," Graham said. "There are reasons why we don't go there. Why the guides don't follow spirits beyond the walls."

"You're not helping," Selena said. "And it doesn't matter, right? We can't be killed."

"There are worse things than death in Riven," Katherine said.

"We have to try, don't we?" I said. "Holing up here does nothing."

Graham and Katherine shared a glance, their faces shifting from concerned frowns to resolute lines in light of each other's eyes.

"Carver's right," Katherine said. "As much as I don't like it, we gain nothing by sitting here."

"We'll make the trek," Graham echoed. "Just know it won't be easy."

"You mentioned an army of spirits?" Nicholas asked me. "By my count, we have significantly less than an army here. Even if we make it to the Mountain, I fear we would face impossible odds."

"I think Inman's group took care of some," I said. "And they drew attention. They made a big burning flag and stood beneath it. If we can find a way to get close to the Master without him knowing, then we might have a chance."

"And if you get rid of him, then the spirits go too," Graham said.

"So that's the plan?" Anna folded her arms, leaned against the wall, all skepticism and spice. "We march off into the woods, Carver and I stop at the border, and then we hope the three of you can take care of the Master by yourselves?"

"Four of us, I believe," Nicholas said. I looked at him, raised an eyebrow. "It's time I acquired some field experience. After all, my inventions are only capable of solving the problems that I know of. And quite frankly, I'm running out of problems to solve."

"Any objections?" I asked.

"So long as I'm not the one taking care of him," Graham said. "We find the Master, he's mine."

"I'll watch Nicholas," Selena said. "I don't want any part of the Master and his sword. I've already been cut enough for one existence."

We gathered up our things and started the long walk towards the city wall. We went west, through the factory district known as the Tar Pit. Where not long ago we staged a series of fights against Graham, trying to stop him from doing what the Master wanted. To stop him from killing me and opening a way back to the real world.

On the way we avoided the scatter-shot sparks launched into the sky by guides on patrol. Avoided breaches and their angry spirits when we could. Graham and his hammer, Katherine and her batons, Selena and her cleaver, Anna and her mace, and my lash. Nicholas, behind us, carried a large pack holding gadgets that I didn't understand. He called them his experiments, and told us to be patient whenever we asked what one did.

After several hours we reached the border, the long wall that circled the outside of Riven's city. Unlike the crumbling buildings, it stood strong and solid, several stories high. Kept intact through some force of will that none of us understood.

The gate was open, a wide archway beckoning us to the forest beyond. I could keep going, but if we stayed in Riven too long, our bodies back in the real world would deteriorate from hunger, or dehydration. Like sleeping for days. There had been more than one guide that had spent too long in Riven and found themselves unable to cross back, their body desiccated and dead back home.

"Straight west for another day or two, and then curl north," I said. "You should be able to see the Mountain and then find his tunnels. Find the Master and end it."

"We won't fail," Graham said.

"Always confident," Katherine sighed.

"Life's more fun that way," Graham replied.

"Says the man who wound up enslaved to the guy we're trying to kill," I said. "Try to make it back alive, all right?"

"Alive? Carver, we're well past that." My mother gave me a wink.

Behind us, Nicholas exploded. I saw it in my mother's eyes, the sudden burst of color over my shoulder. The lights arcing up into the sky and then breaking again and again. Nicholas threw the bursting device onto the street. The rest of us ran to the sides for cover as the device, a small cylinder, eventually stopped spitting the sparks into the air.

"I'm sorry, I'm sorry. It's all my fault," Nicholas exclaimed, running over to us. "It's my panic button. Useful if we were ever under grievous attack. It copies the same spark pattern of a group of guides under assault."

"I noticed," I said. "That means all of you had better run."

"Run?" Anna said.

"Nicholas called every guide within miles to the spot," I said. "If they're still here, we'll have to explain why we've got a bunch about spirits armed to the teeth marching out of the city."

"I'd be interested to hear that explanation," called a voice from down the block. I looked, heart sinking, and saw a squad of five guides staring at us. "Because breaking our laws means a blinding, or worse."

Chapter 11

Friendly Fire

I stepped out in front of my friends and held my arms wide so the other guides could see I wasn't hiding anything. "We're taking them to the Cycle."

"Taking them?" the leader of the squad said. The five of them spread out to cover the avenue, their leader front and center, holding a pair of vicious serrated blades. He stared at me from behind his mask, vibrant red with blue flecks. "I didn't think we were in the escort business."

"These spirits are special," I said. "Too dangerous to let go."

"Is that why we saw the panic sparks?"

"An accident," I said. "Nothing more."

I heard movement behind me. Not good. If Graham or Katherine decided to get hotheaded, then guides would lose their lives. Lives we couldn't afford to waste.

"So you've bound a few spirits," the guide said. "Breaking one rule. Now you're allowing them to draw arms against other guides, a violation of another. And you've called us off our quota to come save you from nothing at all."

"You're taking this a bit too seriously, don't you think?" Graham said from behind me. "We're going about our own business. Business that's nothing to do with you and yours."

"Graham, shut it," I said.

"Your spirit has a mouth on him," the guide said, then pointed at Graham. "How about we strike a deal. You wrangle that spirit right here, now. Then we let you go and don't report this."

"That's not going to happen," I said. "For your own good, turn around and don't look back."

"We heard rumors of guides falling away," the leader said, shaking his red mask back and forth. "Enslaving spirits and doing terrible things. I never thought those rumors were true, until now."

"Carver, I don't think he's going to let us go," Anna whispered.

I didn't want this. We should be fighting the Master, not other guides. But I had to choose, and the Master took precedence. I couldn't let this unlucky band of guides stand in our way.

"Don't kill them," I said. Loudly. I rushed the leader. Took three steps, pulled out my lash and snapped it forward as I came within range.

The guy brought his serrated swords in line, catching the lash in one and trying to hack at it with the other, but I pulled the lash back, yanked the sword out of his hand and flung it to the other side of the street.

On my left, I saw Anna and Selena shape up against another guide holding a thin rapier to go with an arm-coating thick cloth. Meant to take the brunt of a scrambling spirit's attack and facilitate a quick counter.

Graham and Katherine lined up against the other three. Standing between them and Nicholas.

"This isn't your fight," I said. The guide in front of me shifted into a stance, leaning forward with both hands around his remaining sword.

"It is now," the guide spat, and then he charged. I cracked the lash again, this time slipping it between his legs and wrapping around an ankle, sending the guide sprawling. He tried to roll out of the fall, but I yanked the lash back, tightening the grip around the ankle and sending his roll out of control, leaving him sprawled at my feet. I looked down at him.

"End it," I said. "You won't win."

The guide growled at me and made a grab for my ankle, tried to sweep my leg out and send me crashing to the ground. Only I'd seen that move a time or three. Back stepped out of reach. He started to get up, and then I pressed the point of my long knife to the top of his head. He froze. the first good sense he'd shown.

I glanced left, keeping the point of my knife steady, and watched Selena and Anna go through their awkward tango with the rapier-wielding guide. Selena's cleaver didn't give her the reach to get close, but she moved to the guide's side, drew her attention from Anna circling the other way with her mace.

"Why would you do this?" the pinned guide said. "With all the problems we're facing? Why now?"

Anna charged at the back of the rapier-wielding guide with her mace. It looked good until, as Anna swung her weapon, the guide rotated and shoved her shielded arm in the way. At the same time the guide stabbed towards Selena with the rapier, forcing her back. Or at least, that's what I expected to happen.

Selena, her left-hand empty, reached out and grabbed the rapier and yanked it by the blade out of the guide's hand. Selena's palm bore a brutal gash, but the guide, weaponless, held up her hands. If I were human, a cut like that would've hurt, would have ended my ability to use that hand until it healed. For Selena, the cut would vanish in an hour. An annoyance and nothing more.

"What we're doing," I said, "is trying to stop Riven from becoming worse. You have to believe me."

On my other side, I saw Katherine and Graham dispatching their guides. Using the hammer, the blunt side rather than the spike, Graham kept two of the guides at bay while Katherine blitzed the third with a dizzying array of jabs and swipes. Too much for the man's large ax to handle. Three swift strikes to the man's stomach and Katherine swept her legs low, tripped him and knocked the guide over. The ax clattered to the ground.

"I have to believe you," the guide said, a low laugh bubbling up through his lips. "I don't have a choice, do I? If I resist, you'll kill me. You kill all of us."

"We're not going to kill you. We just want you to leave us alone."

Before Katherine could get to his side, the two guides facing Graham charged. One, a burly man with a large metal spear, came in point first. His partner, a lithe figure bristling with knives, feinted in. Graham swung his hammer to stop the spear wielder's charge and didn't catch the knife thrown by the other. The blade embedded itself into Graham's shoulder as his hammer collided with the spear, knocking both of them away.

I saw the blue spark, the pale fire ignite from the lithe guide's hand and trace along a wire I hadn't seen, speeding towards Graham's body. Only my father moved too fast. He dropped the hammer, reached across his chest and, in one smooth motion, drew out the dagger and threw it back at its owner. It struck in her stomach as the fire ran down the link to the hilt, the blade, and over her.

I left my hostage, stuck the knife back in my holster and ran towards the guide. The burly man, who dropped his spear, met me there.

"I'm taking it out," the man said reaching for the knife. The blade still glowed with the fire, the blue burning along her body.

I knocked his hand away and instead twisted the small device around her wrist, the source of the wire that plugged into the knife. The fire went out and dwindled away along the length of her. "Withdraw the knife, you might hurt her even more. What she needs now is to cross back."

"We're not close to our home," the burly man said.

"Then run. Carry her and go."

"Carver," Anna said from the other side of the street. "Are we letting them leave?"

She said my name. Up until that moment, there was a chance that we hadn't been identified. Guides didn't see each other very often, at least not outside of Riven. Names weren't well known, faces were often hidden by masks. Now, there would be no dodging this mess. Unless we killed all of them.

"Let them leave," I said, banishing that dark thought. "We're not here to kill guides."

The burly man didn't hesitate, grabbed his fallen friend, hefted her in his arms, and ran away down the street. Back towards the center of the city. The other guides grabbed up their weapons, and followed. The leader, the one that I'd had kneeling beneath my blade, turned back to me after he'd put some distance between us.

"Carver Reed," the guide said. "You are a traitor to our order. And I'll see to it that you pay for this."

"I can catch him," Katherine said.

"Let him go." I waved her off. "It doesn't matter anymore. The Master is the only thing that does."

But my words didn't do anything to melt the block of ice forming in my stomach.

Chapter 12

The Wrong Side

We left them at the gates leading out of the city. Left them with instructions to keep moving on, to go out into the forest and find the Master. To finish him and stop this mess. What I didn't say, what I didn't tell Anna, is that they might not have much time.

I rode the train downtown, got off at Union Station, and had my hand on the door into Ezra's when I felt a tap on my shoulder.

"Haven't seen you in a while, Carver," Opperman, the newspaper reporter who, in his gray suit and thin, newspaper-branded, mask said. "I'm guessing you've been busy?"

"Do you read your own stories?" I replied.

"No, I only write them," Opperman said. "What do you think? Is Riven going to explode? Are we all doomed?"

"Probably. Know what a breach is, Opperman?"

"Isn't that where a lot of angry spirits come out at once?"

"It's like an infected wound. One that bleeds and spreads its disease out from the sore," I said. "If it's not treated, it spreads and eventually you die. A breach is like that. And Riven is getting full of them."

For once I left Opperman speechless. Trying to find a way to turn my words into a headline. So I left him and walked into Ezra's purifier. But before I shut the door, Opperman raced in behind me.

"Just once," Opperman said, "I think I'm going to need more from you than a line. This is a chance, Carver, a chance to really tell people what you do. Why they should care."

The purifier sucked out Chicago's dirty air and a moment later the inside to Ezra's stood in front of us.

"Nobody wants to know," I said as I stepped into the bar. "They can't do anything about it. You'd be adding another nightmare to their lives."

"We could stop killing each other," Opperman replied.

I would've laughed at the idea. The thought that guides simply saying a bunch of dead spirits clawing back into the real world could end a war. Piotr, and my former mentor Bryce, had been trying that already for years now. It hadn't worked. It never did. The enemy in front of your eyes made an easier target than the one in the shadows.

Alec sat at our table, and not alone. Two other guides stood up as I walked in, their coats a lighter cast than mine, and I recognized their names and faces. From Detroit, not a far train ride away.

"Carver, please sit," Alec said. "You know why they're here."

"Because they wanted to give us a visit?" I replied.

Polk and Derringer, those were their names. Polk a wiry man with a penchant for stroking his wispy beard every chance he got. Derringer an athlete, strong and a fan of talking like it. The number of times I'd heard Derringer shout loud agreement with anything Piotr said, well, let's say it'd been a running game between Alec and I. Bets to see how often we'd hear his bellowing roars of approval.

"You're breaking rules," Derringer said. "They exist for a reason, Carver. Just because you're the head of Chicago, doesn't mean you get to disregard our principles."

"And even though you think you're right, doesn't mean you are," I said.

"Nina nearly died, Carver," Alec said. "As it is, she's in the hospital over there in New York. Serious internal injuries."

At least she'd lived. Whatever they were planning to do to me, if the guide Graham had injured hadn't survived, it would've been much worse. "They attacked me."

"With good reason," Polk said. "What were you doing with all those spirits anyway? Planning something sinister, no doubt."

"What does it matter?" I said. "I'm assuming Piotr told you to come here?"

"I said we wouldn't need them," Alec said. "But Piotr insisted. Said that you would resist."

"What do you think Alec? Should I? Should I resist?"

"We're going to blind you," Derringer said. "Keep you from doing this ever again. So yes, resist. It would make it more satisfying."

I kept my eyes on Alec. Watched his face. He knew all about Graham and the others. Knew about the Master, and what we were trying to do. I could tell he didn't want any part of this. When his eyes met mine, I shook my head slightly. No need for him to sacrifice himself here. If they blinded me, then Alec would be the only one who could take my place. Find Selena, Graham and Katherine. Continue to fight.

"You've got a deal," I said, and made a break for the door. Blinding meant cutting off my access to Riven. Burning away what allowed me to cross over. Polk and Derringer weren't going to take that from me.

I heard a loud crash from behind me, Derringer swearing.

"Oh, I'm so sorry," Opperman said. "Always so clumsy before I've had my first cup of coffee."

I shut the door to the purifier behind me. Stuck my mask on, and ran out onto the streets of Chicago. A fugitive from my own friends.

Chapter 13

Outlaw in
the City

I ran at random. Trying to get away from Ezra's. I took a turn left here, right there. Gradually heading towards the lake, but otherwise without a destination. A problem with being a guide is that you don't make many friends. At least, not those outside your own field. As my field wanted me out, I had to look elsewhere.

Which left two places: the construction site, with Anna and the sneaks. I didn't want to cross into Riven from the construction site, because I didn't have any equipment there. I'd be in the Warrens without a weapon, at the mercy of any guides or spirits that happened to be waiting. I needed to get back into the clock tower and get my things out.

My second option would bring me there.

I figured Alec and the others would be watching the trains, so instead I looked for one of the motoring taxis drifting through the streets. Small vehicles with benches on the outside and slat roofs over the top in case of rain. Downtown, the things ran on tracks laid in the streets. Tracks that funneled electricity up through their wheels. All part of the efforts to reduce pollution. Farther out, near my apartment, larger oil-burning buses were the norm.

As a taxi trundled past, with only one other person on the opposite side, I took three steps, reached out and grabbed a pole and hauled myself into a seat. Leaned over the long console in the middle of the taxi and plugged in my stop by setting a green pin into the map of downtown Chicago. The map's edges were the limits of the taxi's coverage.

My pin would be the second one on the taxi's journey. I'd been lucky. The other passenger had placed his destination in the same direction. His black pin marked the first stop, and only blocks from my target. I sat back and thought.

It would take Alec, Polk, and Derringer time to cross over. Time to let everyone know that I had fled their attempted capture. Alec would doubtless be given my position as Chicago's lead guide. They might give Anna a pass as she'd been inducted less than a day. The other guides we fought wouldn't even have known who she was. I hoped Alec wouldn't go after her either.

I had to keep the other guides from blinding me. So long as I could cross to Riven, my binding on Katherine and Selena would stay. Keep their spirits sane.

I needed to evade capture long enough for my parents to take care of the Master. After that, well, I could take it one problem at a time. Go into hiding and find a better plan.

Maybe I'd turn out like Inman and the others; living outside the city and crossing over on my own vigilante efforts. Help the guides from the shadows. It would mean losing some comforts, sure, but I would still have Selena. There would still be us.

It took an hour, but the taxi eventually trembled to a stop on the street corner I'd been waiting for. I got off, looked up and down the block. Didn't see anything. The sidewalks their usual deserted. The small yards left to their own scraggly weeds. Whatever could grow in the grime. Nobody would be outside at this time of the morning. Everyone either at work or indoors; anywhere you weren't breathing in the terrible air.

I had tried it once, on a bet from Bryce. The goal being that I could take more than three breaths without coughing. I had lasted one. Drinking in the air around here felt like inhaling dry mud. Thick, grainy, and tasting of a million disgusting things. So I kept my mask on, and its respirator did its job.

I knocked on the door; a deep brown oak number in front of a two-story house. Brick and quaint. Squashed between a pair of similar buildings. The kind of home I wouldn't have minded owning one day, assuming I lived that long. I expected to hear the patter of feet, the yelps of children, but there weren't any.

Right. School.

When the door opened, I saw my mentor's tired face. Sad and bent.

"Get inside," Bryce said to me. As I stepped by him, he peeked out the door and looked up and down the block. "You weren't followed?"

"I don't think so," I said. "I moved fast, and I don't think Alec really wanted to catch me."

"I don't know," Bryce said. He shut the door and the house's purifiers kicked into action. "He came by this morning. Earlier. Told me what happened. He thinks you've gone too far."

"Too far? He was there. He fought Graham."

"He won't risk his life for you. Here, take off your mask. Let's get you downstairs. Where you can't be seen."

I followed Bryce through his house and down a flight of stairs below the ground. Through a room packed with boxes and a large furnace with a pile of wood nearby. Summer heat left it unlit, the iron cool and dark. A bed for one sat in a back room, surrounded by clutter.

"What do you mean?" I said as I looked around.

"Alec 's been with the guides longer than you," Bryce said. "Depends on them for his lifestyle. I'm not saying it'll be easy for him, but if it comes between you and everything he knows and depends on; I'm sorry Carver."

"What about you?"

"I'm retired," Bryce gave me a grin that died almost as fast as it came. "But I can't risk my family. You can stay here for now. Not forever."

"You should know," I said. "We know where the Master is. Graham and the others, they're going for him right now. This whole thing could be over soon."

"That's why I brought you down here," Bryce said. "I figured you'd want to cross."

I looked down at the bed. A wimpy frame, a small mattress. Not what I expected from the man who'd been Chicago's lead guide for over a decade. "This leads to the clock tower?"

"It doesn't look like much," Bryce said. "But it will get you there. Before you ask, the reason it's down here, in the basement? My wife came down every morning I crossed to check, in case something went wrong. To keep my children from finding their father's body."

Chapter 14

You Can't Go Home Again

My eyes opened in the clock tower, the center chamber a mix of wood and stone with a line of beds on either side. The weapon rack in front holding my lash, my long knife. For the first time waking up in here felt wrong. Like at any moment I could be attacked by a fellow guide. By Alec. My sanctuary was one no longer.

These were odd hours for our region. Noon back in the real world, when most of our hunts happened at night. I took my gear off the rack and left the clock tower without interference. Made it past the fountain without any guide seeing me. Spent the next half an hour ducking through alleys and avoiding the occasional sparks launched into the air from groups of guides on patrol.

I wondered if sneaks felt this way; always watching over your shoulder and looking around corners to make sure you weren't about to be caught by a guide or torn apart by an angry spirit.

As strange as it had felt to wake up in the clock tower and feel like an intruder, going into the building Nicholas, Graham, Katherine, and Selena had occupied felt even stranger. Nobody home. Devoid of any of the spirits for the first time in months. Nicholas's machines were still there on the first floor, quiet and cool.

I wandered through my parents' place on the second floor; it was utilitarian. Arranged to provide maximum sight lines to entrances and exits, and they had placed a ladder alongside the balcony, one that could extend all the way down to the ground. Ever ready in the case of an emergency.

Checking to see if they were home, that's what I told myself. If they'd already come back from fighting the Master. Or maybe failed to find him and returned. Except, I knew they wouldn't be there.

I'd come to the apartment because it might be my new home. Without the clock tower, I needed a base. The apartment, with Selena, my parents, and Nicholas made the best candidate.

I made my way up to Selena's balcony, where we shared so many hours talking and watching the shiftless sky. Watching the sparks break over the city roofs. I wanted to try something I'd never done before. Something I'd only ever seen with my life hanging on the edge of ruin.

Barth, the mad guide that had tried to kill us in his tower, he'd talked to the Master from a distance. Had a whole conversation in a room without the Master even there. Graham, about to kill me on top of Riven's wall, had been ordered to stay his hand from afar. If the Master could do it, then why couldn't I?

I didn't know how to start. I didn't have instructions, no easy option like flicking on a light switch. Or humming a song. Instead, I tried to find the missing pieces of me. The parts that I had given to Selena, to Katherine, to Nicholas to keep them sane. The connection that bound me to them.

The hollow parts weren't hard to find. Like a tongue feeling for a missing tooth, or sore throat that had disappeared. An expectation reflexively looked for but not found. And that missing tooth or sore throat, each one, each missing piece had a spirit tied to it.

I found Nicholas first. The connection tying the two of us together feeling cool and distant. Like stumbling on a new bump on my skin in the dark and not being quite sure where it was. Only, when I pressed, focused on that feeling, shadowy sensations came back. As though touching something through a cloth. Nicholas's experiences at that moment; his temperature, his emotion, the sense of the world around him. Perhaps I could reach through the other way.

"Nicholas," I said.

I spoke the word aloud, and, as much as I was able to, tried to press it through the connection. Thought the word at the link between us. Then I felt the shock. The flare of surprise come through our bond.

"Can you hear me?" I sent through. Another wave of surprise. Then a pause. Followed by frustration. "Try to talk back."

I waited. Felt the frustration growing in our link. And then it died away entirely, faded to a calm. What was he doing? I opened my mouth, about to speak again, when I felt a chill rush.

"Carver?" I couldn't hear her voice, at least not in the usual way. She came through more like a sensation. Like when you imagine someone talking to you in your head. "Where are you?"

Selena had figured it out. I latched on to her voice, or my rendition of it.

"I'm back at the apartment. Can you hear me?" I asked.

This time, instead of frustration, I felt the warm glow of happiness. Surprise mingling with a smile.

"I can," Selena said. "In a way. Are you all right?"

"I'm better now," I said. "It's been a rough day. Are you making progress?"

"We're still in the forest, but moving fast. We can see the Mountain now, whenever the branches clear up enough for us. We should be there soon, Graham thinks."

"I'm sorry I can't be there," I said.

"I wish you were," Selena replied. "But it's nice to know I'm saving you for once."

"I could get used to that."

I listened to her describe the forest, talk about how the group was getting along. The four spirits venturing on. Graham getting more annoyed with Nicholas every time he stopped to try another experiment. Katherine playing mediator. Selena, well, she was enjoying the chance to explore. To get out from between the crumbling canyons of the city for a little while and see something new.

I don't know how long we were talking, sending our words over miles and miles, but it ended when the apartment door swung open. It ended with a voice I knew saying my name.

"You shouldn't have come back here," Alec said. "If I couldn't find you, then I wouldn't have to kill you."

Chapter 15

Deals Amid Disaster

I didn't say anything to him at first. Instead, I focused on sending one last message to Selena.

"I've got to go," I said. "If you don't hear from me again, I love you."

"Look at this, now you are talking to yourself," Alec said.

"I can still reach them." I turned to face my friend. "Just like Graham and the Master."

"So you are the same now?" Alec said. "You will start getting the same ideas? Binding more spirits? Find guides more loyal to you than our order?"

"You know I wouldn't do that," I said.

"I do?" Alec mused. "We fought to save your life, Carver. To keep this world and ours apart. Now here we are, on opposite sides. Do I chance everything by playing nice? Walking away? I feel like the risk we are taking is letting you live at all."

"Think about what you're saying," I said. Scrambling here, trying to keep Alec talking. My back leaned against the railing of the balcony, a thirty-foot fall to the ground. Alec stood between me and the door. No easy way out.

"Prove me wrong," Alec said. "I am begging you, friend. Show me a better path."

"You have to trust me. We're almost there."

"If you are, then may the guides damn me for what I am about to do."

He ran at me, those gauntleted fists of his swinging low. No time to bring out the lash. I grabbed the knife and stabbed forward as Alec closed. But the guide jumped, grabbed the frame of the balcony opening, and swung his feet at me as my knife stabbed air beneath. The kick knocked me into the railing, almost threw me off. I ducked as Alec swung for my head.

He missed with that one, but the right hook was just a feint for a left. Alec's metal fist connected with my kidney, an organ that didn't exist in Riven, but that hurt all the same. Alec grabbed me as I started to fall back over the railing, and threw me into the apartment. I bounced off Selena's table and landed hard against the wall.

Every time my back hit something, I felt the pressure along my spine as the crossbow shaft jammed against it. This time, that jarring ache gave me an idea. Alec walked in towards me, slow.

"I do not love this," Alec said. "This is not fun."

"Great, I was real worried," I muttered. My right hand grabbed the hilt of my lash. I stood up, stared Alec straight in the eye. Ignored the nausea coming up from my rollicking stomach, the bruising ache from my back.

"I promise you," Alec said. "After this, I will continue your hunt for the Master."

"Aren't you a regular saint." I raised the lash, and Alec flipped the table towards me. Launched it with both arms. I shifted my shoulder to block it and the table pressed me to the wall. Alec came after. A series of quick jabs into my side.

I rolled away and Alec let me escape, let me get some distance. If I'd been a spirit, or someone he truly hated, those gauntlets would've kept pounding me until I was nothing more than mush.

"Who told you?" I asked. "Who gave the order to blind me?"

"Polk and Derringer were at Ezra's when I arrived," Alec said. "They told me it came from Piotr. Hours earlier."

"Piotr didn't want to talk?" I once again had my back to the balcony, Alec advancing towards me.

"He is a busy man," Alec said. "Enough of this, Carver. It's time to go."

Alec darted forward, the same run-up to a punch that I'd seen him do a hundred times. I flicked the lash towards his feet, to the left. Alec moved fast, jumped over the strike, only I wasn't aiming at him. The lash wrapped itself around the leg of the table and I pulled it tight as Alec came through the doorway to the balcony.

The lash's cord swept up through the doorway and caught Alec's ankle. Tripped him and sent him flying into the railing. I ran back through the other way. Slipped the lash back in my holster and reached over my shoulder to pull up the crossbow. Locked in an orange bolt as Alec picked himself up and turned towards me.

"You know what this can do," I said, leveling the crossbow at Alec.

"You would burn down this building," Alec said.

"I don't exactly have a lot to lose."

"What is your offer?"

"Let me leave. You can say you didn't find me, we can forget this happened," I said. "Then, after I deal with the Master, I'll come back and you can blind me."

Alec stared at me for another moment. Weighed the options. Nodded. "Go. But I will keep looking for you. Next time I won't be alone."

I didn't give him a chance to change his mind. Ducked out of the apartment, ran down the stairs, hit the ground floor and dashed out into the streets. Like Chicago, I went at random but always with one general direction in mind. I had to make a stop, and then I would have to cross back. I had no doubt Alec would be waiting at the one place I could do that.

The clock tower.

Chapter 16

Immolation

I watched the clock tower from the top room of a building across the courtyard. Looked right over the fountain at the guides standing in front of where I needed to go. Three of them, and Alec stood in the middle.

Crossing out of Riven meant tying yourself to a location. My body, my real body, sat in Bryce's basement. That bed linked to this location in Riven, the clock tower. Every time Bryce crossed from that bed, he would appear in the same place over here. It's how we managed to keep our equipment where we needed it. How we determined which regions guides around the world would patrol.

It wasn't all that hard to find a new place to cross over from the real world. You needed somewhere you could fall asleep. Some guides were so good, so able to relax on any floor, that they could cross in and out anywhere. That didn't work for me, but maybe I needed to rethink my comforts. I'd never been able to cross over without a cushion or a mat. Somewhere safe. Getting *out* of Riven, though, only had one option. Had to go out the same way you came in.

That meant the clock tower. Finding my bed and crossing back. I didn't think Alec and the other guides would just let me by without a fight.

But I hadn't come empty-handed. My lash, my knife, I'd left those back in the Warrens. Where Anna and Laurence crossed over from their hideout beneath the construction site. A place, so far as I knew, Alec and Bryce didn't know existed. The one thing I'd brought with me?

The crossbow.

The orange bolt loaded from the fight with Alec was still ready for action. I went over to the crumbled wall that faced another street, out of sight from the guides in front of the clock tower. Aimed the crossbow at a house half a block down.

My shot zipped across the street, struck the building, and burst into orange fire. The blazing rays climbed up and down the house, and leapt towards the buildings around it, spreading into an all-consuming nova. I backed up, glanced out towards the clock tower, and saw what I'd hoped for: Alec and the other guides running across the courtyard towards the blossoming burn.

As they passed by my spot, I dashed down the stairs and sprinted across the courtyard. Behind me I heard their shouts, Alec calling for them to search the nearby buildings and keep their distance from the fire. At the entrance to the clock tower, I took a second to look back. To make sure Nicholas's invention wasn't going to roast the entire city.

It looked like solid spiderweb, orange burning lines lancing from place to place, connecting with stone, wood, or wandering spirits and flaming into a new nova. At the edges, though, the intensity faded. The jumps were shorter. The lines smoked and died. I hadn't destroyed the city to make my escape. At least, not entirely.

"It was an ugly block anyway," I said to myself as I slipped inside the clock tower. I shoved the crossbow beneath the bed as I jumped in it. Not that I expected it to remain hidden, but I could use any minutes they spent not knowing I'd already crossed back.

I closed my eyes, and drifted back to Chicago.

Chapter 17

Saved by a Sneak

Bryce's basement had no lights, felt like midnight, even though I knew it was only mid-afternoon. I curled out of the bed and felt my way to the stairs.

I took the steps up slowly, testing each one for creaks. Bryce had given me a chance, and I didn't want him to die for it. Or suffer. The sooner I left his house, the sooner he could claim I'd never arrived. The sooner his family would be free from the risk I carried with me.

I heard thumps from the front door, exclamations of welcome from Bryce and his wife as their kids came home. I took the opportunity to slip from the basement and head back to the kitchen. Went by the nook where, not long ago, Bryce had told me about his quest to find my mother. Back when things had seemed so much simpler.

Out the back door, my fingers catching the metal frame as it closed to muffle the noise. An empty lawn, a plot for a garden that would never grow. An alley where, every so often, crews in large trash tanks would trundle by and collect the refuse. Only when I lost sight of Bryce's home did I give myself a chance to breathe. To take in the summer weather filtering through my mask and beneath my coat.

I'd taken one step towards my new life. Now came the second.

The construction moved fast. When I first came here months ago, there had been piles of steel bars and a plot of land. Now a frame loomed seven stories high. Powered winches and pulleys shoved material up and down, back and forth, while workers sporting various equipment welded, tied, or measured every new piece. A foreman stood at the base with a monoscope, flipping through the various lenses to zoom in on his team's activity and shout out instruction.

Nobody noticed, or bothered, to call out my presence as I walked behind them. I slipped around the edge of the construction site and headed down a steep set of stairs. The door had a knocker but I ignored it. Twisted the handle and went straight in.

I strode down the main hallway, beyond a pair of rooms that were always closed off, and into the center chamber. Dominated by a big table with scattered bits of food and drink on it, the room drew my eyes to its walls. To the maps hanging there, outlining parts of Riven in detail ranging from perfect to light sketches and theories. Candles burned. Still no electricity down here.

I reached inside my front coat pocket and drew out the map taken from Mead's cabin. Unfolded it and tried to find where, if, it matched the ones on the wall.

"You ever think to knock?" Laurence, Anna's partner and a generally unappreciative fellow, said to me as he walked in the room. "We're not your apartment."

"Now you are," I said. Laurence looked confused, which was the point.

"They kicked you out?" Anna said, following her partner to the room. "We were waiting here, like you said. But I didn't think they would actually do it."

"The rules are clear," I said. "Hurt another guide and you're going to get blinded."

"You didn't hurt her."

"Graham did," I said. "Close enough."

"He's my spirit," Anna replied, drawing a questioning look from Laurence.

"Don't say that," I said. "If they don't know, then they can't come after you. I've already taken the fall."

"That's the first smart thing I've ever heard you say," Laurence said.

"Someday, Laurence, we'll be friends."

"Hey, you give me a weapon like hers, I'll call us good," Laurence said. "Till then, you're just a guy that shows up and gives me grief."

I went towards the wall, towards the map of the forest that hung from the back. Held up Mead's map to it. They were close, but the sneak's map had more detail. More symbols.

"Is this your map?" I asked Anna, she shook her head.

"It's mine," Laurence said. "I do the exploring, Anna handles the clients. What do you have there? You draw a map of your own?"

I relayed the story. The kidnapping on the train, the ambush attempt on the Master. Anna had heard most of it before, but it was worth taking the time just to see Laurence's eyes bug out.

"On my way back, I found this map. That's how we know where the Master is," I said. "You've got more on your version. Like this one spot, here."

I pointed to the large red circle, directly on the path between the city and the Mountain. Shaded in with the words *avoid at all cost* next to it. Laurence came close, put his finger on it, humming to himself.

"Yeah, I remember what that is," Laurence said. "It's a ghoul. A real old, nasty one. I studied it for a while, kept out of sight. Seems to stick to that area, which is why I drew the circle."

"It's right on the path," Anna said. "They might walk right into it."

"The path to the Cycle?" Laurence said. "Because that's the route you're looking at. It's why think the ghoul's there in the first place. Plenty of spirits walking by, and it snaps them up."

"Wait," I said. "You're saying the Cycle is in the Mountain?"

"I mean, I've never seen it," Laurence said. "But I've come close. Tracked enough spirits to see them go into those caves and never come back out."

"It could be on the other side," I offered, and Laurence shrugged.

"Maybe. I'll tell you right now, you go anywhere near that ghoul, you better be ready. It's not normal."

"We have to warn them," I said to Anna.

"How?" Anna replied.

"I've got a new trick to show you," I said. "Let's cross."

Chapter 18

Cut Off

The Warrens. A miserable mess of sprawling apartments, crumbling buildings, and lost spirits. If you wanted to hide, the maze made for a good spot. We crossed over into the basement of one of those buildings. A six-story monolith bland in every way except for its height. We didn't wake up in beds, instead I stood up from a mat with ratty pillows on the ground.

"This place could really use an upgrade," I said, stretching out.

"Oh, I'm sorry it's not up to your standards. I'll get right on that," Anna replied.

"You should," I said. "The better your site is, the easier the crossings get. If you're under pressure, every bit of comfort helps."

"Why would we be under pressure? Oh yeah. Because now every guide in this place is hunting us."

"You should be used to that."

Sneaks weren't exactly targeted by guides, but if they found Anna skulking around and talking to spirits, guides would take care of her. They would give her a choice. Give up her location in the real world and get blinded. Or die, right there and then, for interfering with Riven and the spirits of the dead.

"I thought my sneaking days were done when I became one of you guys," Anna said.

"I thought they were too."

Anna led me to the top of the building. I didn't know whether or not height would make things easier, but we could see farther. Had a better chance of noticing any guides before they got to us. If we had to, we could run and the guides wouldn't know where we crossed from. We had to keep our exit hidden. I didn't have a crossbow anymore, didn't have a good way to create a distraction so we could dash by and cross over to the other side.

Anna watched as I reached into myself and felt for those missing pieces. As I tried to open the channel between Selena and I. Last time, I'd felt the wave of emotions coming back through. The rush of feeling and sensation, like a breeze on a dead wind day. Only now I felt nothing. As though my mind ran into a hard wall. I tried Nicholas, my mother, and they were the same.

"I'm not getting them," I said. "Try Graham."

I walked her through it and Anna closed her eyes and concentrated. A minute later opened them, shaking her head.

"Nothing," Anna said. "I can feel where he should be, that part of me that isn't there, but when I tried to connect with it . . . I couldn't feel anything."

"I don't know what that means," I said. "They might be dead. Cycled. Or maybe a guide found them and they've been wrangled apart from us."

"Wouldn't that give us back the parts of ourselves?" Anna asked.

I nodded. The sneak had a point. Those parts of me were still missing, which meant Selena and Katherine and Nicholas were out there still. Stuck in that forest somewhere.

The forest. A place we couldn't get to. Unless . . .

"I have an idea," I said. "We're going to have to take a little trip."

Chapter 19

To The Rails

For the second time in years I rode on a train heading outside of Chicago. This time, nobody pointed a gun at me. Much nicer sitting with Anna and watching as the city trailed off into grain-filled fields.

"Have you ever been out here?" I asked her.

"Plenty of times," Anna said. "Sometimes clients write me. Or wrote me, I suppose. They didn't want to come in the city, so I would go out to them."

"Quite the service," I said.

"We charged them for it."

"Did you ever feel bad?" I asked. "Taking advantage of people's grief?"

"Do you ever feel bad sending people to oblivion?"

"I didn't ask for this," I said. "But no, it's my job, and it's a necessary one."

"That's how I felt too. If people want closure, and I can give it to them, then why shouldn't I?"

Another time I would've pushed her on that point. I would've made an argument about how it's harder for people to move on if they think about the one they lost wandering in that desolate wasteland. Hard to get over disaster if they think they could still, maybe, have one last conversation with that person. But I didn't. I stayed quiet and let Anna have her moment out the window.

Who was I to define right and wrong?

An hour later the train pulled into the station. The last one of the day, the sun setting over the bluffs. It felt familiar, like when I came there last. Only this time there weren't any horses. No gruff former guides waiting to escort me up into the wilderness. Just Anna and I walking along the road.

Some people spared us a glance or two, but, like in the city, people preferred to pretend we didn't exist. Carriages called out to other passengers to ask if they wanted rides and ignored us. Even some of the horses shied away as we walked past the posts.

Once we were away from the station and walking the path that led towards the bluff, I pulled off my mask. Anna followed suit.

"I wondered when you were going to do that," Anna said. "I feared I'd forgotten some rule."

"The air is better out here," I said. "But if you've been reading the papers, listening to the people, there's a lot of disease. We're not immune to that."

"You're paranoid."

"Cautious," I replied.

We continued up the path, going up and around rocks and underneath the wide trees. I kept scanning the canopies for the bats, those funny creatures flitting in the twilight. So unlike birds with their spastic patterns.

"Carver," Anna said, her voice in a whisper. "I think there's someone up there."

I followed her pointing finger. There were lights ahead. Not the flickering of a campfire, but electric. Plenty of them. I nodded towards the side and Anna went with me into the brush. We moved slow, stepping over ferns and between the scraggly branches of newly grown trees, but if anything came up or down that path they would have a hard time seeing us.

At least eight uniformed policemen and their horses stood in the campground. Poking around and loading the rigid bodies into carts. I don't know why I didn't think of it. Of course a massive die off out here in the woods would attract attention.

I reached in my coat and felt the hilt, the metal of Inman's pistol. Not that I had any kind of experience with these things, but I worked with the weapons I had.

"You're not going to fight them," Anna said.

"I don't want to," I said. "I think if we wait, they won't stay all night."

"You want to just sit here?"

"I don't see any other option."

We hunkered down beneath a large bush, bugs swirling around our heads, and watched as the officers continued digging around. Calling to each other whenever they found something interesting. I laid my head on my hands, and watched as the sun finished its descent and plunged the forest into night.

"Hey," Anna whispered. "I think they're gone."

I open my eyes. Stunned for a moment. I'd actually fallen asleep. Taken a nap. Probably for the first time in years.

The lights were still there, electric lamps set up and plugged into a large boxy battery. The lights illuminated a sign that said *Keep Out— Active Investigation*. Beyond that, beyond the ever present wildlife, there were no noises.

"Keep your eyes on the ground," Anna said as we moved closer. "They'll have triggers to keep animals away."

"You've done this before?"

"Not everything we get paid for happens in Riven," Anna said. "I learned how to get around."

"Remind me to stop underestimating you."

We made our way to the campground and over to the cabin where I crossed over not two nights ago. Where Inman's body had been. The police had replaced it with a chalk mark. A small note saying a body had been here.

"This is it," I said. "If we cross over here, we'll be in the forest."

I told her to take the bed that I'd gone in. I slipped into Inman's. I didn't know precisely where I'd cross over, but I figured we be able to find each other. Either that or we'd be arriving alone, without weapons, into a forest full of danger.

Chapter 20

Where the Spirits Walk

I awoke under the gray grim trees. Those black leaves shaded the pale light, casting dark shadows all along the dead ground. The breeze blew, rippling through the branches, adding a lifeless chime to the place.

There were some marks on the ground, flattened parts of broken stems leading towards the clearing. I followed them, hoping Anna would do the same. Before long I'd returned to the same spot where I'd seen Inman carved in two, where so many former guides had fallen. The scars were there. The black lines running up and down the trees, weapons scattered about along with the occasional bit of cloth. Pieces torn from guide coats and masks. Otherwise, there were no bodies. Riven didn't have those. Not for long, anyway.

I'd seen it happen before. A guide falls and, in the aftermath, their bodies slowly disappear. Their spirits awaken elsewhere in Riven. Or sometimes right on top of their corpse. As the energy faded, so did the body, and the spirit started its walk to the Cycle.

"You weren't lying," Anna said as she stepped into the clearing and looked around.

"You thought I was?"

"No," Anna said. "I guess not, but your story sounded strange. A bunch of guides massacred by an army of spirits and a crazy villain wielding a giant sword?"

"For Riven? That's almost every day."

"For you, maybe. At least now we have weapons," Anna said. The sneak had a point. We had crossed over empty-handed, all of our gear far away in the Warrens. There were plenty of weapons scattered around the clearing and I didn't think their former owners would mind us taking them. We both fished around for something we knew how to use.

In the middle the clearing, I found Inman's two pistols, his long knife and a pile of spare bullets. Not my favorite weapons, but the guns were small enough to take along. I slipped them into my pockets. Took the knife and then found a longer sword on another body. No lash, but I could use the edged weapons.

"Check this out," Anna said. I looked her way and saw her holding what looked like a long chain with handles on either end. Along the length of the links were tiny spikes, serrated edges meant for cutting. "What do you think?"

"That doesn't look easy to use," I said. "And tonight is not the time to learn on the fly."

Anna shrugged, "I'm going to take it."

I helped Anna find another couple of knives to slot in her belt and then we looked around. There weren't a lot of markers for where to go. If I remembered Mead's map correctly, then the Mountain stood northwest of here. The path the others had taken would be straight north.

"I agree," Anna said. "How can you tell directions? There are no stars."

"Look," I said, pointing towards one part of the clearing. The grass there was decimated, trampled under more pounding feet than any other part. "If most of the spirits came from that way, and the Master lives in the Mountain, then that would be where we want to go. We just follow the tracks."

Anna didn't argue, and we set off through the woods. Anna played with the chain. Practiced whirling around, and nearly took my head off once or twice. Still, I'd rather she knew what to do with it when the time came.

It felt like hours, but without any moving sun or changes in light, it was impossible to tell time in Riven. Eventually, in front of us, a crowded line of spirits appeared. They walked, blank-eyed and without speaking, through the forest. Towards the Cycle. Ghosts shifting through the trees.

We came to the edge of the path and watched them. The long line of soldiers, sick patients, and normal men, women, and children in a long walk towards the last moments of their existence. Wandering Riven, you saw people of every color and background, every race and origin. Some crossed over covered in tattoos, or piercings, while others wore elaborate headdresses and spiritual robes.

I'd never seen them all at once. Never noticed how many hundreds and thousands of spirits must be walking this road every minute of every day. How few must be losing their minds in order for us to keep Riven safe.

"It's almost beautiful," Anna said, her eyes running down the line. "All of them, from all these different places and they're all at peace."

"For now," I said. "I never realized. If all of these spirits turned, there would be no way. No way we could hold them back."

"The world is a big place."

We watched for a while longer until, shaking my head, I pulled Anna between a pair of dead-eyed soldiers and we made it to the other side of the path.

"Let's keep walking along. If I remember right, on Laurence's map, that circle is somewhere up ahead," I said. "If anything took Graham and the others, it would be that."

"You think we can fight it?" Anna said. "Us? Alone?"

"Alec and I fought ghouls and won," I said. "Anyway, we don't have a choice."

"Oh, that makes me feel better," Anna sighed.

We marched along with the spirits, matching their steps and staring off into the woods, looking for any sign of our friends.

Chapter 21
Big Game

It wasn't hard to see where Laurence's red circle began. Off to the side of the path, to our right as we walked alongside the spirits, was what looked like a giant hollowed-out tree. A stump as tall as the other trunks in the area. Its open-air top a ridge line of broken bark reaching up towards the sky.

"What do you want to bet that's where Laurence found the ghoul?" I said.

"You're the expert on these things," Anna replied.

True. While I hadn't hunted many ghouls—the first one only came with Alec a few months back—you could spot the telltale signs: torn up sections of Riven, a lack of angry spirits, and a general sense that you were not where you should be.

"What's messing with me is that ghouls normally crop up when there are bunch of angry spirits in an area," I said. "All of these spirits are passive. Or they've been wrangled by a guide back in the city."

"Do ghouls age?" Anna said. "Does anything age in Riven? Maybe there used to be spirits here. Laurence said he thought the ghoul looked old."

The sneak had a good point. Riven didn't seem to change all that much, except the slow deterioration of its buildings. A crumbling as much to do with the fighting between angry spirits and guides as any sort of natural force.

"It's possible," I said. "Normally anything big enough to get noticed gets taken care of quick."

"I'm saying we don't know what this thing is," Anna said. "If we try to think that this is something we've seen before, it could be a bad idea."

"So be ready for anything."

We left the spirits behind and walked up to the stump. Searched our way around its base. The stump's bark a fading brown, unlike the gray forest. Patterns and textures lined the wood, unlike the featureless trunks of the other Riven trees. Whatever had once grown, whatever had produced this stump, had been something unique.

"There's an entrance," Anna said. She walked a few steps ahead of me, around a curve in the stump. I followed and looked. Saw something less an entrance than a torn hole. Jagged edges and splintered chunks of bark surrounded a space twenty feet wide. Light vanished into that hole, bending into the ground.

"This seems ominous," I said.

"We crept into a campground full of bodies, looted the weapons left over from murdered guides, walked along the trail with thousands of other spirits, and now you're saying this, this is the ominous part?" Anna said.

"I stand by it," I replied. "Never walked into a tree before."

"We're both getting a lot of firsts today."

We took those first steps through the entrance into the stump. My hand drifted towards my belt where, normally, I'd have a sparker. Something to shoot light out in front of me. Without one, we descended into the dark with only the faintest glimmer of reflected gray following us.

The air changed as we went down, thickening and growing pungent with the smell of rot. An unusual smell in Riven, where souls didn't decay. Something lived down here. Or had lived.

The pathway stayed wide enough that Anna and I could stretch our arms around us and not hit an edge. That didn't give me a lot of confidence. I preferred any monsters to be smaller than me. Strange how rarely that happened.

The ground beneath our feet changed over from dirt to polished wood. Only, as I knelt down to feel the smooth ground, it felt like rock flattened by ocean waves through years and years of pressure. The kind of stones you would find on a beach, smooth and clean.

Just as the last bit of light winked out behind us, we saw a flicker in front. A whisper of a glow sneaking out around a bend. We followed it, taking each step slower than the last. Noises, the shifting growls and grumbles of a large creature making the most of its next meal echoed their way down to us.

"I didn't think ghouls had to eat," Anna said.

"I don't think this is just a ghoul."

When we turned the corner, I wasn't thrilled to see I was right.

In front of us, bathed in the light from a hole in the stump's roof overhead, hung a gnarled mass of roots, plants, and bodies. Spirits ensnared in vines and branches, a roiling ball linking to the outsides of the stump through veins of wood and pulsing green stems. The sphere sat suspended in the center of the stump, like a marble caught in a spider's web.

As we watched, the thing moved and shifted. Morphed and sent bits of itself crawling up and down the stems, arms and legs reaching out and being drawn back. Occasionally a face appeared, small and rough in the mass, but always with its mouth open in a wide and silent scream.

"Of all the horrors in Riven," I said. "I've never seen one like this."

"Laurence wasn't lying," Anna said, her voice devoid of feeling, in total shock. "I don't even know what to call this. What it is."

"Wait, look closer." I could see along the sphere, along the stems that held the ball up, there were cuts. Deep gashes and burns. Wounds suffered in a fight, and some of them still dripped bits of phosphorescent goo onto the ground. "It's hurt."

"Graham." Anna straightened, looked at me. "I feel it. The part of me that I lost."

I followed her words. Felt for my own connections, that piece of myself long since given to Selena. And found it. For the first time in years, my body and soul were whole. Which meant . . .

"They're gone," Anna said. "That's the only way the binding breaks, right?"

I nodded. Selena, I couldn't feel her anymore. She'd given that part back to me. Or had it ripped from her. I gripped the sword I'd taken from the guide's body and drew it from my belt.

"There's only one way to get them back," I said.

Chapter 22

Two Person Job

I took the lead, running into the central chamber with the sword in my right hand and one of Inman's pistols, loaded and ready to fire, in my left. I almost fell. My legs moved faster than before. My muscles felt stronger, lighter. Even my eyes were sharper; I caught the changes in the flickering gray as the beast shifted its tendrils and limbs around, picked out the numerous wounds delivered by our friends.

I was whole.

Not that the ghoul cared.

I didn't see any eyes, but it noticed us. With snapping, crackling noises the ghoul withdrew its connections to the stump. Ripped off the branches and veins until its mass slammed into the stump's floor. Those whipping, swirling tendrils slithered into an array around the ghoul's body, pointing at us.

"That's not good," Anna said. "I liked it more when it was sitting still."

"I'm feeling it's just getting started," I said. "You take your chain and see if you can keep it busy. I'll go for the kill."

Not that I had any idea of the best way to do that. Figured a headlong rush at the center would do. Sink the sword in, twist the hilt, and let the blue fire do its work. I heard Anna shout as she sprinted away to my right, that bladed chain waving through the air. The ghoul turned, the sound of its body grinding against the ground as its waving brown and green mass shifted towards Anna. I took the opportunity to charge.

The ghoul's main body, framed by pulsing emerald tendrils, sat in front of me. The round surface looked like a ball, perfectly round except for where the tendrils emerged. Beneath the surface I could see the shifting faces, arms, and legs as they twisted and turned within.

After seeing the Master's dark cloak and his huge sword, a normal nightmare seemed refreshing.

I made it ten steps before the first tendril swatted at me, a thin vine swiping down from above and looking to flatten me into the floor. I saw it cracking down, twisted and slashed upward with the blade as the vine came streaking towards my head. My sword cut in to the attack, but did nothing to stop it. The vine crashed me to the ground and coated me in goop running from the cut I'd made. The stuff felt warm, sticky. Unpleasant. I felt the vine wrap itself around my chest and with my left hand I raised Inman's pistol. Aimed right at the ghoul's center mass, a target too big to miss. And pulled the trigger.

The gun went off with a roar. The shot popped into the monster's ball, scattering a chunk of ghostly flesh off of the thing. Otherwise, the ghoul didn't seem to care. As the vine lifted me up, I noticed the ghoul didn't cry. No roar coming from the beast. No angry howl. Only the gravelly crackle and whistling wind as its body shifted and moved.

"Could use some help?" I yelled as the vine dragged me through the air. Smaller tendrils branched off of the vine, threading their way between my arms and legs. The plant squeezed, my limbs going numb. My right hand, weaponless, was pinned to my body. I couldn't exactly reload the pistol either. If something didn't change soon, the ghoul would squash me into pulp.

I saw the chain whipping by my face, wrapping around the vine. The chain's edges bit in and cut all the way through, severing the ghoul's tendril and sending me back down to the ground. The vine cushioned my blow, hitting first and bursting into a sticky pile of ichor. I blinked away the slime, amazed to discover that I did, in fact, still live.

"Now it's your turn," Anna yelped from across the chamber. I looked and saw her beating away a pair of vines with her knives, stabbing them as they came close. Above her, a branch shifted into position; straight and hard.

"On my mark, roll left," I said, my hands scrambling to reload the pistol as I came up to a crouch. "Now!"

Anna dove to her left as I fired the pistol. The branch swung to follow, which took it right into the path of my shot. The bullet exploded into the wood and scattered chunks all over the place. The main body of the branch fell down and landed on the twisting vines turning to chase Anna, trapping them onto the floor.

"Nice shot!" Anna said.

"I'll take it."

I holstered the pistol and drew my knife, grabbing the sword off the ground as I ran back towards the ghoul. Two more vines arced towards me, but now I knew how fast they moved, and dodged. I sidestepped their grasp, then planted my foot on the end of one and swiped down with the sword, cutting it off. The vine flailed around, twitching and leaking the same blue glowing goo as the other parts. Every time I thought Riven had run out of ways to be disgusting and horrific, it proved me wrong.

The ceiling shook. The stump rumbled and it took me a second to see why. The ghoul's other branches had rotated up and bashed at the hole, letting in more light and sending chunks of wood taller than me raining down to the ground.

"What's it doing?" Anna said, running over past me towards her chain, a vine trailing after her.

"Running away," I said, no idea whether that was true. So I went after it.

I closed within a few feet of the ball and leapt towards it. As I jumped, wood chunks raining down around me, the ghoul lifted itself towards its new, wider opening. I swung the sword and felt it bite in to the ghoul's skin, or whatever it was. And found myself hanging by my own blade. The stump's ground fell away beneath me and, with a yell, I swung my left arm up with the knife. I stabbed the knife into the ghoul, giving me a second handhold.

The ghoul rose up above the stump, its vines and branches breaking out into the sky and smashing through the canopies of nearby trees. I clung to my blades, keeping my grip tight. I wouldn't be able to hold forever, and if I fell from here, well, Anna would be cleaning up my splattered remains.

The ghoul moved off the stump, shifting over the forest floor, using its branches to stab into the ground and move itself along in lurches. I tried to twist the handle on the sword, to activate the fire, but I didn't have the leverage. Even trying to cut free might cause me to plummet to the surface. My arms burned. I needed to move.

With my left, I went for it. Withdrew the knife and stabbed higher up. Then, with my right, I pulled out the sword. The move sent me swinging back as the ghoul jerked over the dead grass. My left wrist ached, but I held on, and lunged back at the ghoul, sticking my sword in a little higher. For its part, the ghoul ignored my climb as it walked. I took a needless breath, then repeated the steps. Inching my blades foot by foot up the ghoul's body until I reached the top. Until I stood on the thing's head.

And saw where we were.

Beneath us, beneath the swirling twitching mass of vines and branches, was the infinite line of spirits marching towards the Cycle. The ghoul began to feed. One after another, the ghoul scooped spirits up from the path and shoved them into its spherical mass. Pressed them into its skin, even where I'd cut it. Wherever the spirits touched, the ghoul grew larger. The cuts healed. New vines started to sprout.

We were running out of time to beat this thing.

I raised the sword and slammed it down into the top of the ghoul. Went to turn the hilt, when I saw a face in the skin below. Selena's eyes, that vicious scar, they looked up at me blank and unseeing. The sparkle I'd become used to no longer there in her dead gaze.

I hesitated.

The ghoul hit me hard, sent me flying off its head with a thick vine. Small leaves actively grew around me, spreading their tiny tendrils between my arms and legs and wrapping them around my neck.

"You're not playing fair," I said, immediately regretting opening my mouth as more plants shot their way inside. The vine tasted like spinach, full of iron and bitterness. I ground the leaves in my teeth. If the ghoul wanted to tear me apart, well, I'd make it pay. Give it the full power of my gnashing gums.

The vines swung me through the air, suspended me where I could watch as the ghoul continued feeding. As it grew stronger, pressing the helpless spirits into itself one by one. I saw one of the spirits running, catching a vine and riding it towards the top of the ghoul. Just before the spirit smashed into its skin, I saw its arms move, a chain fly out and wrap itself around the vine.

That wasn't a spirit. Anna had caught up, and she cut herself free. Fell towards the ghoul and landed near my sword. As the vine grew leaves in front of my eyes, coloring the world a lighter shade of green, I saw Anna climb over to the sword and twist the hilt.

Blue fire ran down the blade and streaked out over the creature, running down its sides and up its vines and along its branches. I felt my vine shiver, the leaves withdrawing out of my mouth and wasting away. Shriveling to nothing as they held me twenty feet above the ground.

I fell.

Chapter 23
Reassembly

I didn't know the spirits that I landed on, the ones I crushed down into the dirt, but I thanked each and every one of them as I stood up. Around me the unending march continued, only now around this part of the path swarms of spirits stood staring at the trees around them. The lives consumed by the ghoul over its long reign.

"Carver!" Anna said. "Where are you?"

"Over here," I said, not really sure where here was. I looked around, scanning the faces. Before too long, all of the spirits would head towards the Cycle. There were hundreds of them. I had to find Selena. Graham, Katherine, and Nicholas too.

Anna shoved her way through a crew of centuries-old sailors. Their ornate coats contrasting with their swarthy appearance. She looked rough; bruises across her face and more than a few cuts and splinters sticking out from shredded parts of her clothes. Going by the multitude of aches and pains bouncing their way through my body, I gathered we both felt terrible.

"I can't believe we're alive," Anna said as soon as she came up to me.

"Why? We're guides. This is what we do."

"Stop it. This is not what guides do. Guides handle one or two angry spirits in a back alley in the city. They don't attack a giant creature that's covered in whirling death vines and then act all cocky about it when they luck their way into victory."

"I don't know what you're talking about," I said. "I left the sword there for you. I knew you'd get to it."

Anna stared at me, mouth open and her head shaking. "If my hand didn't have at least three splinters in it, I'd smack you right now."

"Have to save your energy anyway," I said. "We still have to find the rest, bind them again, and then cross so we can put ourselves back together."

"No. You wait one second," Anna said. She stared me in the eye, her face fierce. "We did something incredible. You're going to take one sentence. At least one sentence, and acknowledge that."

She was right. The ghoul we'd defeated, who knows how long that thing had been here? How many spirits it had feasted on? We knew it had bested Graham and Katherine, up to this point the deadliest duo of guides I'd ever seen. Anna and I, and let's be honest, mostly Anna had beat the creature through a combination of luck, skill, and determination. I felt bad about doubting her, about insulting her abilities, because she had proved herself one of the finest guides I'd ever seen.

"Any time now," Anna said, picking a splinter from her shoulder.

"Fine. You are amazing. That was incredible. I'm glad we're not dead. Can we go now?" I said.

"I guess that's all I'm going to get."

"You guess correctly."

We spent a long time sifting through the souls. Wandering through crowds of spirits and inspecting their faces. Hunting for familiar outfits. We eventually found them, all four together, beginning to walk at the edge of the crowd.

If you've ever seen someone you loved look at you like you don't exist, then you would understand what I felt seeing Selena. I walked up to her and she turned to look at me. Her eyes met mine and I saw none of her in them. No recognition, no thought.

When I had released Graham from his binding to the Master, he'd retained some of that personality. He'd still been, to some degree, himself. Ghouls were different. They devoured spirits, crushed them into nothing. I didn't know if I could ever get her back.

I had to try.

Anna watched as I took Selena's hand and felt for that pinprick. Felt for that connection to bring us together there in that gray forest. When I found it, I poured myself into her. My body wilted as my energy sapped through our touch, as what gave me life passed through into her. It found a home, and I felt the bond grow. A tether between our souls formed out of mine.

"Carver?" Selena's voice poured like chill water on my face. I hadn't realized I'd shut my eyes, but I opened them and saw her looking back at me. Not the dead-eyed spirit, but Selena herself.

"You're back."

"It feels good," Selena replied, looking down at her hands gripping tightly. "I don't remember any of it. Nothing after the ghoul attacked us. Now here you are."

"I'm sorry I wasn't there."

"It's not your fault." Selena smiled. "I think we almost had it. Graham and Katherine were keeping it distracted while I protected Nicholas. He prepared something that exploded. Or that meant to explode. But we didn't see all the vines."

"It had a lot of those," I said, "and they tasted awful."

Selena raised an eyebrow.

"Never mind."

I bound Nicholas and Katherine again, waking them from their slumber. Anna did the same to Graham and after replaying the fights and the challenges to each other, all of us went back to the stump to retrieve their weapons.

It felt strange, giving up those parts of myself again. I'd grown so used to being without them; always being slower than I should be. Tiring faster. Being my full self had felt good. Maybe someday I'd have that again.

"Carver," Anna said as everyone stood assembled. "We should probably go. Cross back. We've been over here for a long time."

"Can you keep going?" I asked my parents, Selena and Nicholas. They nodded.

"That thing caught us by surprise," Graham said. "I don't think the Master is a giant monster full of vines. We'll take care of him."

"If we can," I said. "We'll try to come back the same way tomorrow night. Meet you at the Mountain."

"I like that idea," Nicholas said. "It'll give me time to study the surroundings. Find a plan."

"Plans," Graham shook his head. "Run in with a hammer held high, now that's a plan."

Anna and I left them to carry on, made our way back past the line of spirits, to the clearing, into the beds of grass and crossed home.

Chapter 24

Police Work

I opened my eyes to the wide black barrel of a gun, and behind it the furrowed brow of a police officer. He wore the standard blue and copper uniform, the metal winding through the cloth around various badges and devices. He gave me a moment, let me collect my breath. I glanced to the right, noticed Anna staring at the weapon.

"Now that you're both awake, I'm hoping you won't mind giving me some answers," the officer said. "It's been a while since I've had someone decide to fall asleep in a crime scene. Particularly when that someone doesn't want to wake up."

"We were in Riven," I said before Anna could get any ideas. "We're guides. We were trying to figure out what happened."

"Guides," the police officer said. "Guides way out here. Just happening to come by after all the others died."

I could've said anything. I could lie; protest that we were innocent and that we'd only stumbled on the cabin as a place to spend the night to complete our quota. Or I could tell the truth, say that I'd been here the night the guides were slaughtered, but all that would get me is an interrogation. Questions about why I hadn't gone directly to the police. So I went with option three.

"It's guide business," I said. "Riven is a mess, and we're trying to clean it up. The group here made mistakes, we came to fix them."

"Did you now?" the officer said. "Why don't you stand yourselves up, and come with us. Then you can tell me all about exactly what mistakes were made."

"Gladly," I said. Not that I had a clue what I was going to say. If they actually checked with the guides about my name, they'd find my fugitive status right there.

"Carver," Anna said. I held up my hand.

"Don't say anything," I said as we got up from the beds and followed the officer from the cabin. "The less you can implicate yourself, the better. If we're lucky, you'll still be a guide after we get out of this."

Several more officers milled around the campground outside. When they saw us come out, one of them took off a pack and reached inside. Pulled out a pair of what look like collars.

"What are those?" Anna whispered.

"Shock collars," the police officer said. "Normally we keep them for sneaks. Anyone who feels like Riven is a place to run off and hide. I wouldn't advise crossing while wearing one of these."

"It reacts to your breathing. If you start to even out, like you're falling asleep, it'll zap you." I said. I'd had a short, ugly experience with those while being trained. A demonstration to show what would happen if you went astray. I had no doubt that Polk or Derringer had one back at Ezra's and, if I'd waited a moment longer, they would've tried to clap it on me.

"You're really ruining this whole guide experience," Anna said.

"Bad timing on your part," I replied.

"Since you're both so talkative," the officer said. "How about you tell me about those mistakes?"

I went into a censored version of the story, spinning a tale about how all of the people here were former guides, how they had tried to break a hole through Riven back to the real world. About how that hole didn't work out. Attracted a lot of spirits. Too many. The guides' own ambitions had cost them their lives.

"Sounds like they were a real batch of evil men and women," the officer said when I'd finished. His deadpan hadn't changed at all. No idea whether he had bought the story. "But here's the funny thing. We and all the other departments around Chicago, for hundreds of miles, received a notice last night. About a guide who'd gone his own way and refused the justice your kind insists on delivering itself. Included in this notice was a description. One you happen to resemble. It also included a note about a mask. Black and gold. I think you'll agree that the one you're carrying there holds those colors."

The officer clapped the shock collars are on each of our necks. They felt tight, cold. Every time I swallowed or took a breath my throat scraped against the metal.

I saw Anna's eyes flicked towards me. Shook my head slightly. Four officers, two of us. We might've been able to win, but there are some things you don't come back from. Binding spirits, even injuring the guide in Riven, those were different. Here in the real world, these officers had family, friends. A blinding, getting cut off from Riven forever, still meant you were free. Not locked in a prison cell.

"It sounds like you've already made a decision," I said.

"Maybe I have," the officer said. "I think you'd better start walking. On the way there, back to the station, you're going to give me the real story. Because right now I have a cart with twenty bodies in it and no one to tell me how they got there."

"You're not going to understand," I said.

"Trust me," the officer replied. "I long ago figured out that this world doesn't provide easy answers. Doesn't give clear explanations. But eventually someone will come around and ask for them all the same. I don't need to understand, I need to be able to say why."

So as we marched down to the station I retold the story. Told him about the man in the cloak with the big sword, and the army of spirits that slaughtered those that had made the camp. The officer took it all without interrupting, and finally nodded when I was done.

"Now that is a story I can believe," the officer said as we walked up to the train station. "Not because it sounds believable, but because the way you said it proved that *you*_believed it."

Waiting at the top of the station's steps were Polk and Derringer, their eyes bearing a deadly glint. Derringer favored his right arm, and when he saw that I'd noticed, shot me a spicy glare. They would be the escorts. Lovely.

"We'll take these two from here, officer," Polk said.

"You should know they've both been cooperative. For fugitives, the best company. Even helped me clean up my investigation."

"We'll take it into account," Polk said. We followed them onto the train and they pointed us to a pair of seats.

"Straight to the hospital this time," Derringer said. "Right into surgery. Your game is done, Carver." Then he turned to Anna. "Too bad he dragged you into this. I heard you had potential."

"Fun while it lasted," Anna replied.

The train blew its horn and started rumbling off, back towards the city. To the knives that would cut away Riven forever.

Chapter 25
Cuffed

Polk and Derringer sat on a bench across from us, staring at me with narrow, suspicious eyes. Their mouth's twitched. Derringer coughed once into his wrist, then returned to his glare. As though they wanted to ask me a question, but were waiting for me to do something first. Me, with a shock collar around my neck and cuffs on my hands.

Guess I'd better get started.

"Seems like a lot of effort for one wounded guide," I said. "They're pulling two of you from your quota just for this?"

Derringer glanced to Polk, giving me their order of operations. Polk could play the lead and Derringer would be the muscle. The ease with which they slid into their roles had me wondering how often they'd done this. Were they Piotr's go-to handlers whenever a guide stepped outside the lines?

"You know what's funny, Carver," Polk said. "We were in Detroit. We were filling our quota. Then Derringer and I, we went to our normal meet up spot. Like that bar you've got in Chicago. Ezra's?"

I nodded. Polk spoke with a bad affliction, a habit of emphasizing the wrong syllables. Like an actor learning how to talk by watching silent films.

"Like that one. Only when we got there, Piotr was sitting at the table. Waiting for us. Now I don't know when last time was you saw him. But to me, to Derringer here, Piotr looked old." Polk widened his eyes, made a helpless shrug. "Looked tired. Like he'd been in a lot of fights. Had a lot of nights in Riven, and a lot of days back here battling for the survival of all of us.

You know what Piotr says? You know what he tells us as Derringer and I sit down?"

"That you're doing a swell job?"

"He tells us that there's this new kid, this guy he thought would make one heck of a guide, would make such a good guide that even though he's only been part of us for a few years that he deserves to run Chicago. Derringer and I, we're looking at each other like hey, we've both been doing our work for more than a decade, and we're not getting anything. But we're quiet. We take it. Because that's what loyal guides do." I could see Polk start to shake. His forearms trembled, hands gripped the bench. Derringer put a palm on Polk's shoulder. "So when Piotr tells us it's the guide that he thought was the next big thing? That the man whose helping us dig out of these dark times, tells us that this wonder kid has gone and hurt one of our own. Has broken our rules. We didn't take long to jump on the train."

"You didn't even ask him why, did you? Why he thought I was doing this?"

"Oh, no," Polk said. "Should we have? Should we have interrogated him? Tried to question the man who single-handedly keeps our order alive? Or do you, you know, give him this one. Seeing as all the evidence is on his side."

"I'm being hunted," I said. "That's why I'm here."

"Who isn't being hunted?" Derringer sneered. "You? Me? All of us got spirits after our hides. All of us are dealing with one terror after another every night."

"You understand," Anna said, "the people coming after Carver aren't like the spirits. They're trying to find him. Just him."

"Why is that?" Derringer said. "What makes you so special?"

Part of me wanted to spill the beans. To say to them that I, by an accident of birth, could be the end of everything. But then, why would they believe me? Why would it matter? If they were going to take me in anyway, then who cared?

"Let's say that I'm not just a guide," I said. "Because of my parents, I can be used by someone else."

"Ain't that mysterious?" Polk said. "Aren't you special?"

"Hear that Polk?" Derringer said. "This guy thinks that he's better than us."

"That's not it," I said. "You have to let me go. Keeping me puts Riven at risk."

"You talk about how you're getting hunted in Riven," Polk said. "Sounds like there's a simple solution for you. We take you back to the hospital. We get you blinded. Then guess what? No more Riven. No more getting hunted. You're safe. Piotr's happy."

"Everybody wins," Derringer added.

I didn't have an argument against that. They were right, to a degree. Blind me, I couldn't be used to create a hole out of Riven. Only, that would still leave the Master out there. Would leave whomever came next at the mercy of his schemes. I couldn't let that stand.

"What about the people hunting me?" I asked. "Who's going to deal with them?"

"Why don't you give us all the details?" Polk said. "We'll take care of it for you. Derringer and I. We'll hunt them down. Send that nasty spirit into the Cycle. Along with those spirits you bound over there."

"Polk, don't take any offense, but you two wouldn't stand a chance against my friends," I said. "If you do blind me, the best thing you could do would be to stay out of Riven for a while. Because they'll find out who cut me off, and they won't be happy."

Polk laughed. "Threats? You're something else, Carver."

"Not a threat," I said. "It's a certainty."

Polk sat forward on the bench, his elbows on his knees. "Know what? Alec? He says he knows all about where you've holed up your pals. Soon as we blind you, we're crossing over and taking care of them. I don't care how good you think your spirits are—they'll be outnumbered. Outclassed."

"You broke the rules, Carver," Derringer said. "It's what you deserve."

Outside the windows, the fields began to pepper with buildings. Streets broke between the yellow and green acres of early summer. Sunlight washed the world in gold.

I wanted to go back to Riven's gray.

Chapter 26

Simple Operation

Dr. Barrington Farth looked the same staring down at me, preparing to cut me off from Riven, as he had when he told me how my mother died; clinical, distant, methodical. Alec had strapped me down into the hospital bed, Anna similarly confined next to me. They called it surgery but the blinding really amounted to a small incision under the temple. Snipping part of the brain.

There were potential side effects.

"It used to be that we would hit you on the side of the head particularly hard," Barrington explained. "As you might imagine, this led to some unfortunate trauma. A higher likelihood of death. This way is rather pleasant."

"You're really selling it," I said.

"Carver, be quiet," Alec said. He stood in the corner, near the door, supervising. To make sure Anna and I didn't try something weird. We still wore the shock collars. Ready to zap us if we tried to escape by going to the other world.

"First you'll be feeling a slight prick as I numb you," Barrington continued. "Then the actual procedure will only take a moment. Simple slice, a few stitches, and you'll be free of your burden."

"You think this is fair," I said to Alec.

"It's not my position. Not my decision to make," Alec said. "I'll let them know."

He meant Selena. Graham and Katherine. Nicholas. That only applied if he could get to them fast enough. If Alec could cross to Riven in time to tell my parents what had happened before, freed of their binding, they journeyed to the Cycle and disappeared forever.

Barrington turned to a small table and loaded a syringe, sticking the needle into a small vial and filling it up with clear liquid. I should have felt panic. Dread. Instead, my mind fogged with the malaise of the inevitable. I'd tried, and I'd failed. I only hoped it would take long enough so that the others could finish their mission. Find the Master and eliminate him before the blinding set them free.

"Hey Alec," Polk called from the hall. "Bryce is here. Says he wants to talk to you."

"I thought you'd retired?" Derringer asked, his loud voice carrying into the room. I didn't hear Bryce's reply.

Alec caught my eyes and shook his head. "He shouldn't have come for you."

Alec stepped out of the room and I heard their voices back and forth. Polk and Derringer interjecting as Bryce protested the treatment. The injustice of my sentencing, that Anna had no right to be included in it. Polk countering that Piotr made the call and, as guides, they had to obey his orders. That's when I heard the punch. A thud in the hallway. Polk's muffled groans echoed into the room.

Barrington turned at the sound, holding the syringe in the air like a weapon, and then the doctor shrugged and backed into the corner of the room. Another pair of strong hits and a yelp from a nurse, and I heard another body hit the floor. Bryce walked in, rubbing his knuckles.

"These new guides never learn how to fight outside of Riven," he said to me as he reached over the bed and undid the straps. "They've got their fancy toys over there, but ask them to engage in an old-fashioned brawl and they fall apart."

"What are you doing?"

"Alec told me what was going on," Bryce said. "I objected to it. There are more important things right now than punishing a guide for a little injury."

"They won't let you walk away from this."

"I didn't want to face my family every day knowing I'd let this happen to the son of the best guide I've ever known," Bryce said. "It's worth the risk."

Bryce pressed the latches on either side of the shock collar, held them down for a full ten seconds. The collar ground as its gears turned. It popped off, one side opening to let my neck slip out. I could have held the release down myself—shock collars normally paired with handcuffs, and the time for the collar's gears to unlock gave guards ample opportunity to intervene.

"I'm gathering there won't be a procedure today?" Barrington muttered from the corner.

"You gather correctly," I said, getting out of the bed and pulling on my coat.

"You'll need to leave the city," Bryce said as he unshackled Anna. "If you stay here, they'll find you. My guess is, after this, they forget about the blinding and go for more permanent solutions."

We walked from the room and headed down the hallway, passed the unconscious forms of Polk and Derringer. Alec watched us, arms folded, as we went by. I expected him to say something, maybe a threat or jeer. Some measure of acknowledgment. But whatever war Alec waged went on inside his head and he stayed silent.

Outside the hospital Anna and I turned towards the train station. The quickest way out of the city. Bryce didn't move with us. He looked north, back towards his house.

"You're not coming with?" Anna asked.

"I'm not leaving my family," Bryce replied. "If they choose to blind me, I don't care. I'm done with Riven anyway."

I held out my hand and when Bryce took it I pulled him into a tight hug. "Thank you, for everything."

"Don't go wasting my gesture," Bryce said. "Leave."

We left my former mentor and ran through the streets. Towards the train station and, hopefully, a way out of town. While not as big as Union Station, the trains near the hospital had some options. One went south, toward St. Louis, and others wrapped east towards Detroit. I kept my mask off, breathing the harsh air and drawing stares, but if there'd been any sort of release about me then going without the black and gold mask would buy me some cover.

"You there," shouted one of the station's policeman, gesturing at me with his baton. "What's your name?"

I glanced around, pushing Anna away for me. Trying to get her some cover. I walked out of the line for the tickets, pretending not to hear. The policeman repeated his question and I kept moving. His whistle blew and I ran. Back up the steps and out onto the sidewalk. I coughed, my rapid breathing pulling too much harsh air for my lungs to cope with. I jammed on the mask, started the respirator.

The officer lunged at my back and I felt him grab my coat. I twisted with the move and shrugged him off, sending the officer tumbling to the ground. Three more were heading my direction, pounding up the station steps. So I took off.

The streets around the station showed signs of a new age for Chicago. Wooden stores and offices were being torn apart to make room for forged metal. Ever present construction. Small zeppelins carrying materials bobbed overhead, guiding people and beams to their proper places. Shifting crowds of workers in the late morning moved their mass of bodies along the streets or in the automatic taxis. Every so often, as I darted between crowds, I caught sight of one of the city's mechs, the tall two or four-legged beasts that, with stacks belching smoke, rumbled their way on patrol.

I burst through the crowd and found myself in a large intersection, bustling groups crossing in shifts to blue and red signals on ten-foot posts. At random, I went left. Down a long sidewalk that stretched in front of a row of offices claiming various legal representation. The kind of office I could probably use right about then. In front of me, as the block ended, a black metal leg pounded into view. Followed by another.

The cockpit of the mech, a half oval with a glass windshield set over the top, a pair of large guns beneath, swiveled to point my way.

Its barrels trained on me, and I paused. Raised my hands.

"Carver Reed," the mech announced, the pilot's voice catching a mechanical twist coming through the machine. "You're under arrest, and any action taken without our consent will result in your immediate execution."

Chapter 27

Get Outta Town

Anna grabbed my shoulder and pulled me into an alleyway. Out of sight of the mech. Then she continued, yanking me further with a vice-like grip on my wrist

"I can run on my own," I said, trying to break my hand out of her grasp.

"Then do it," Anna said, but she let me go. Anna kept moving, taking a right at the next break between the buildings and bursting out onto the street behind the mech. Running across the road, darting between a pair of taxis and into another alleyway.

I followed, wheezing through my respirator. To say I didn't go on too many runs was an understatement. Exercise came in fits and starts. Workout sessions to hone techniques with Bryce. Push-ups on the floor of my apartment. There weren't other options.

"Where are we going?" I asked when Anna finally took a second to breathe.

"The airfield," Anna said.

"I thought you were getting train tickets."

"They were watching the trains," Anna said. "The officers had pictures of us. There was no way would we get on one."

"Oh, but a zeppelin's going to be so much easier?"

"If we're lucky." Anna took off again.

We broke onto a large thoroughfare heading west. A wide street with multiple taxis, surging crowds, and plenty of police hunting for us, their blue and copper masks bobbing between more common outfits. Anna kept her head down and ducked between groups, trying to stay out of the open. I followed suit, except there were some things the shorter, smaller girl could do that I could not. Like be inconspicuous.

"I've got them!" a voice bellowed behind me.

"You're the worst," Anna said.

"You could've just left me there," I replied as we broke into another run. As mechs turned to track us and the officers chased, we kept swerving in and out of people. Trying to prevent any clear shots. It worked, at least for a while. We made it three blocks up before the constant whistles and cries of alarm cleared the streets.

When a mech spools up its gun, it sounds like a strobing whine. A clear signal you're about to be torn to a million tiny pieces. I caught up to Anna, grabbed her, and jumped into a storefront. Smashed through the glass windows as the sidewalk blew up in gunfire. Sparks flared behind us, bullets bouncing into the street and through the window that we'd crashed to pieces. One advantage of being covered with a coat and mask is that the glass didn't manage to cut us. Some new scratches on our clothes, but no blood.

"That's a neat trick," Anna said. "Adding vandalism to our charges?"

"We're still alive, aren't we?"

"Can't argue with that," Anna said and we took off towards the back of the store. It was full of dresses and shirts, blouses and pants. The people inside ran behind the sales counter or ducked in the racks of clothes. Anything to get them out of sight of the two crazed people fleeing through their store. Behind us officers came in through the door, yelling and blowing their whistles.

We blew through the rear, past rows and rows of clothes that didn't make it to the front of the store. Clerks stared at us as we went by and I repressed the urge to wave. Not the best time. We went out the back door, into another alley.

"This way," Anna said, turning right and running parallel to the wide street we'd nearly been killed on earlier.

Another block down the alleyway and I heard officers behind us, catching up. We did our running in Riven, these guys did it here, in the real world. Where their muscles gave them one heck of an advantage.

"Need a new strategy," I gasped as our feet pounded pavement.

"Here," Anna said. She cut into the back of a restaurant. Right to the kitchen where serving staff and chefs were prepping for dinner meals. I followed, banging against pans and pushing people out of the way. I thought I muttered apologies, but I couldn't be sure. Chaos navigated by instinct. Trying not to die.

We ran out through the front of the restaurant and onto a smaller street. Anna swung left, then dove in between a pair of buildings heading back the way we came. Anna slowed, crept to a crawl as we went down the alley. Hid behind a large bin for trash and watched as groups of officers ran by. Chasing after our trail.

"Won't they think we're heading for the airfield?" I said. "Given that's where we were going?"

"We weren't," Anna said. "The main airfield's that way. The one we're going to? It's much smaller. South."

I'd heard of that one. A few flights a day to major cities. Only luxury class zeppelins, the ones that would take longer but gave you a scenic route. A chance to really enjoy your time above the clouds.

"We're escaping on the slow ships?"

"Wasn't aware you were on a schedule," Anna said.

That stopped me for a moment. I supposed I didn't have anywhere to be. Waiting for Graham, Katherine to go and take care of the Master. Until they succeeded? I just had to survive.

"Point."

"Okay, let's go," Anna said and we ducked back into the wider alley and shot down the road in the opposite direction we'd started. This time, when we hit the crowded street, there were far fewer officers. None of them scanning our faces. Why pay attention for fugitives when they'd been on the run in the opposite direction?

It took another hour of walking but we made it to the South airfield. There in the center, on a giant cleared patch of grass, sat a zeppelin as large as a football field. Its numerous fans spun in the wind, idly keeping the zeppelin in place. Long ropes tied the craft to the ground as people boarded. They walked up a long stair connected to a platform with wheels at the base. A series of uniformed officials took tickets and welcomed everyone on.

"So I'm guessing you have the money for this?" I asked Anna. "Because I didn't plan on buying cross-country air tickets today."

"We won't need it," Anna said. She made a beeline for the ticket counter, for one line in particular. One man who looked at her with beady eyes when she stepped up in front of him and smiled.

"Calling in the favor?" the man asked.

"Time to get out of Chicago for a while," Anna said. "You have room for two of us?"

"With the war, there's plenty of space. People don't seem to like leisurely travel when the world is falling apart."

"Imagine that," I muttered.

The man stamped out a pair of tickets and handed them to Anna. Wished us a pleasant trip. I waited until we passed the pair of officials checking tickets, until we walked on the aircraft, to ask what that whole conversation was about.

"If a client can't pay," Anna said. "I ask what else they can do. Whether there's something that might come in handy later. He said that he could get me a free trip on one of the ships in exchange for doing him a favor in Riven."

"Not a bad deal."

The zeppelin's inside matched Ezra's classical charm. Ornate woodwork and long, electrically-lit hallways glowed with warmth. Mustard carpet matched the deep brown doors and walls, and room numbers carved in polished bronze hung above every cabin. We traced our way past a series of dining rooms, a small library, and a wide viewing gallery with windows on every side and even a large glass section in the floor.

"Ever been on one of these?" I asked Anna. She shook her head. "Me neither. Maybe, when we're not being hunted, we can try this again. Actually enjoy ourselves."

"You guides ever get to do that?" Anna said. "Enjoy yourselves? Because everything we've been doing since I joined has been risking our lives in one way or another."

"You have to find the moments."

"Next time you see one, mind letting me know?"

We reached our cabin and Anna put in the key, twisted it in the lock, and opened the door. A pair of beds nestled against the walls in an otherwise spacious room. Windows everywhere looked out onto the field. When we were in the air, those let us see in every direction. A bottle of wine nestled on a shelf in the wall, with glasses. Snacks littered an accompanying table, cheeses and sausages. A note welcomed the passengers to the luxury cabin. Anna's contact had more than come through.

"Anna?" I said. "This is one of those moments."

Chapter 28

Luxury Life

Amid the cabin's opulence, my eyes focused on the two most important things in the room. The beds. As soon as we were both in the cabin, I shut the door behind us and locked it. Our friends were getting towards the Master and, if we wanted to find them, if we wanted to help them, we had to move.

"Do you think the beds are linked?" Anna asked.

"The ship looks new, so I'm hoping no," I said. If nobody had used the beds to cross to Riven before, then they would be untethered. Open. Anna and I would be able to focus on a particular spot in Riven and cross there. From then on these beds would be tied to that spot forever. Of course we could try to use the floor if the beds didn't work, but you still had to be able to fall asleep. Waking up from a long session in Riven on a hard surface usually meant a stiff body, a day spent regretting the night before.

"So what's the plan?" Anna asked, lying down in her bed.

"I say we visualize the stump. The only place I can picture to that's going to be closer," I said. You couldn't just name a spot in Riven and go there from an untethered bed. You had to know it. Be able to guide your spirit there as it crossed over.

"The stump it is then."

I lay down on the bed, took off my mask, and stared at the ceiling for a minute. Officially a fugitive. On the run from both guides and ordinary police. On the off chance they searched the ship while we were in Riven, they would take us in without a fight. Lock us up and, assuming we were even able to cross back, we would find ourselves in cells. On the other hand, if Selena and the others needed help and we sat here too nervous to do anything, then everything was worthless. Then the whole sacrifice, the injured guide, would have no benefit.

We had to hope that there was nothing coming for us. That our luxury cabin would kiss the skies without police dragging us out of it. I heard Anna's breathing even out as I closed my eyes. The last time we crossed we'd nearly been killed. This time wouldn't be any different. We were going to find the Master and put an end to this.

Chapter 29

To the Mountain

We joined the spirits making their way from the stump. That long crowded stream of souls of every shape and form marching towards the Mountain in the distance. Again, we were weaponless. A problem to solve when we caught up to the others.

I relished the calming walk through the forest after the rapid-fire sprints from the officers back in Chicago. So long as I didn't focus on many dead, the quiet walk let me relax. The leaves shimmered in the breeze and neither of us spoke. Took the opportunity to collect ourselves.

I tried at one point to reach out to Selena and I felt her, sent some reassurance through our bond and received her warm response. Not frantic, not scared. They weren't fighting anyone yet.

The Mountain rose gradually on the edge of our vision, hazy through the endless waves of gray and floating ash that made up Riven's air. Eventually, though, we hiked up to the entrance. A portal cut into the side, perfect and spaced twenty yards wide to allow the spirit throng through. Graham, Katherine, Selena, and Nicholas were waiting.

"You didn't try going in?" I said.

"We did," Graham replied. "Explored a fair bit. Even found some of these."

Graham waved behind them. A pile of various weapons and robes, cloaks and coats sat there. Most of it looked like guide gear, but old, cracked and torn through use. Some bore versions of the guide's symbol in different sizes, some etched or stitched with simple fabrics. Rather than the thick leather that made up most of our new gear, a number of these were made from thin cloth. Almost rags.

"What does this mean?" Anna said as she sifted through the weapons, looking for something she could use. "None of this stuff looks standard."

"It means that the guides weren't always in Riven's city," Katherine said. "Or someone, sometime, brought this out here."

"The spirits that the Master sent to murder Inman, they didn't have weapons," I said. "They were smart, but just used their hands and mouths. If he had these available, why not use them?"

"I have a feeling they're meant for others," Graham said. "This one, for instance." Graham pointed at a particularly vicious-looking sickle whose point carved into a forked tongue. A serpent's ridged scales made up the rest of the curving blade. "That's the same sort of weapon that Rainier, one Chicago's first guides, wielded. Might even be the same."

"Why would it be here?"

"Things don't age in Riven," Nicholas answered. "It's possible that someone found it. Collected the weapon and brought it to the Mountain. Or even that Rainier died and left it here."

"There's one person that'll be able to answer those questions," Selena said.

"Selena makes a point," Graham said. "We're here. We're ready. Let's do the job."

I picked up the sickle, and a shorter sword. Longer than the knives, and broader, but the two felt good in my hands. Anna, for her part, found a simple mace with spikes jutting out of its head. Similar to what Nicholas had made for her.

Then, with me in the lead, we joined the line of spirits and headed down into the Mountain to find the Master.

And end him.

Chapter 30

The Old Ones

We hiked through the opening into the Mountain, the yawning gray rock closing around us and blocking out the sky. Deep down the tunnel, past the ends of Riven's gray light, blue flickered on the walls. The same pale cast that burned in the eyes of angry spirits and lit up our weapons when we attempted to send that anger into oblivion.

"Where do you think it's coming from?" Anna asked, nodding down the tunnel. Spirits shuffled by us, continuing on their journey towards the Cycle.

"Take a look around you," I said. "It's coming from where they're going."

"This would be the proper location for the Cycle," Nicholas said. "If the Cycle is indeed in the base of the Mountain, then that makes the Mountain and all of its rock the only thing holding the Cycle at bay."

"If the Cycle is something that can actually be held," Katherine said. "I've never seen it."

"You might get your chance," I said and then kept walking. I'd never been in a cave before. At least, not the natural kind. Chicago had plenty of underground paths, but they were made of metal and stone. Weren't traveled by an endless mass of spirits.

As we went into the cave, the air itself became clearer, Riven's ashy haze didn't reach far into the depths. Outside light vanished, replaced by the blue glow. It reflected up and down the cave walls, their shiny surfaces serving as mirrors to the sapphire cast. Every so often a path branched off to the side, and every single time I glanced at Graham and Katherine and they shook their heads.

"That's where we found the gear," Graham said after the first offshoot. "Every one we explored ended with a small circle and a cushion of leaves and grass. Weapons and coats lying next to them. The closer to the entrance, the older the gear."

"It sounds like people crossed over here," I said.

"My impression as well," Nicholas added. "There is evidence that the guides once used the Mountain as a base."

"But not anymore. No guide I know has ever been here. Most probably don't even realize it exists."

"Why would you need to?" Graham said. "All the fun is back in the city. These spirits are long past needing our help."

Eventually the cave opened into a large chamber with a central flat, rocky space. Around that circle, the spirits continued walking a sloping stair into the depths. The circle held one thing that made me pause. Towards the back, against a wall, sat a makeshift bed, scattered sheets and a ragged pillow. The great sword I'd seen the Master wield hung behind the bed, a pair of spikes pounded into the rock serving as a rest for the sword's hilt. Next to the bed, on the ground, lay his same hooded cloak.

"I think we found him," I said.

"Except he's not here," Selena replied. "Only, why would a spirit need a bed?"

"It means the Master is not just a spirit."

We surrounded the bed. For being such a deadly figure, the Master didn't live in luxury. The clock tower I'd used for years in Chicago stood in gilded contrast to this spartan existence.

"So what do we do now?" Graham asked. "Wait?"

I almost said yes. Almost said that we ought to stand with our weapons drawn so that when the Master crossed over we could strike before he had a chance to blink. But the scraping noise of a sword drawn from its sheath drew our attention. Had us turning as a group towards the downward stair and, on it, a spirit wearing nothing more than a ragged robe, holding a long blade I recognized from other guides on the opposite side of the world: a katana.

"Those weapons do not belong to you," the spirit said.

"You are?" I replied.

"Takeda," the spirit said. "Former leader of the guides. And destroyer of thieves."

Then Takeda, destroyer of thieves, ran. Dashed down deeper into the cave, pushing past spirits and disappearing.

"You remember your history?" Graham asked.

"Takeda lived two centuries ago," I said. "I don't understand how he can still be here."

"I say we go ask him," Graham said.

We split up; Graham, Katherine and I resolving to chase Takeda down the steps while the others watched the Master's bed. I figured they would be able to handle the Master as he crossed over, taking shape defenseless on that pile of cloth.

The three of us ran after Takeda, circling deeper into the bowels of the Mountain. The blue light brightened to the point where it almost hurt my eyes, forcing me to squint until they adapted. I pushed past spirit after spirit as the path tightened. Narrowing until only two bodies could move abreast. The ceiling shrank, brushing the top of my head and forcing me to duck. And then we found it. The source of our salvation and our ultimate end.

The Cycle spanned an immense space in front of us. Its radiant blue spun off as far as I could see and beyond. A lake of churning cerulean aura. In front of us, forward on a flat expanse that trailed into a single point, walked the spirits. They moved to the very edge and without breaking stride walked off and fell into the Cycle. Takeda watched them, katana still drawn. Next to him stood an even older spirit with nothing more than a long staff and a plain tunic. Together they turned to us as we walked in.

"Do you find it beautiful?" Takeda asked us. "You should, as you'll be sinking into it soon."

"I've seen better," I said. Which was a total lie. If you could stare into the sun, and the sun were as big as the sky, then you might understand what it was like to see the Cycle up close. I had to focus on the ground, focus on the spirits, because staring at that blue meant sinking into it and never coming back.

"Tell us," Katherine said. "How are you here? After so many years?"

"We will not honor the thieves with answers," Takeda said. He nodded at the other spirit, who turned his face towards us. Some terrible fate had torn the spirit's face away, the mouth a mangled mess. Nose broken off. His bones were charred black.

"Zolin," Graham said. "Leader of the guides back in 1500. A monk. His temple burned and destroyed by Spain as they made their way through Mexico. With him in it."

"So now there's two of them?" I said. "Both former leaders? Both far older than any spirit should be?"

"It's a troubling coincidence," Graham said. "One I think we can rectify."

Graham pulled his hammer off his back, held his gauntleted wrist ready. Katherine drew her batons, and I raised the sickle. Really wished I had my lash. My knives. Going up against some of the best guides that it ever lived, I'd rather do it with weapons I knew how to use.

"Are you ready?" Takeda said. He pointed the sword, that long katana, at us. Countless spirits walked by, oblivious to the world around them.

"Let's go," I said, and ran forward.

Chapter 31

Duels

Graham made a beeline for Takeda, while Katherine split off to engage Zolin, leaving me with a choice. Which parent did I love more?

Easy. Graham had tried to kill me so many times; my mother deserved my help. So I slipped by a soldier's spirit, pulled ahead of my mother, and swept the sickle forward to meet Zolin's swing. Zolin caught the strike on his staff and wrenched the sickle away from my hand. My weapon flew across the room and bounced off of the cave wall. Zolin's disarm swept his staff wide, leaving room for me to stab him with the sword. The blade stuck into

Zolin's side and he replied by whipping the staff back and knocking me away.

I bowled into a trio of spirits and sat up to see my mother battering Zolin, my sword still sticking out of his body, with her batons. She drove the monk back with a flurry of blows, each baton running a rhythm of strikes up and down Zolin's body. I noticed that my mother took special care to strike my sword as well, driving it deeper. Desperate, Zolin dropped the staff, ignored my mother's batons as they clawed into his arms. He grabbed my mother and threw her to the ground.

"That's not fighting fair," I said as I tackled the monk. I gripped one of my mother's batons, sticking in Zolin's body like my sword, in my right hand and drove it into the wasted space of the monk's mouth. Zolin groaned, more a buzzing whine without a tongue to shape the sound, and flailed as I pushed him back towards the edge of the platform. I stuck my leg behind Zolin's, and sent him tripping back over the edge. As he fell, I reached with my left hand and snagged my mother's other baton. The short sword fell with Zolin into that blue oblivion.

"Carver! Look out!" Graham called. I whirled back and held the batons up in time to catch Takeda's blade. The katana came at my face, and bounced off the batons. The force threw me back, my feet brushing the edge of the cliff. Takeda readied for another swing when I saw my father's hammer slam into the spirit's back and knock Takeda to the ground. I shifted away from the edge, gained some distance. Graham bore a number of deep cuts along his arms and legs. Takeda hadn't gone down quite so easy.

Graham reached the spirit and, as he grabbed his hammer off the ground, Takeda turned with a sweep of the katana, swiping towards Graham's stomach. As the katana swept up, Graham fired a burning wire from his wrist. It wrapped around Takeda's hand and lit on fire. The spirit dropped the katana and howled in pain. Pain that my father, with a two-handed swing of the hammer, put to rest.

Both of us pushed the motionless Takeda off of the cliff, into the Cycle. Two guide legends erased, and neither one gave us any answers.

"Disappointing, isn't it?" said a voice behind us. A voice I knew. Cloaked and holding his sword at his waist, point touching the ground, stood the Master. His obsidian mask shone in the Cycle's blue light, still chipped from Inman's desperate shot. "They've been down here for so long that they've lost their edge. Nothing more than pitiful memories."

"How did you get here?" I asked, trying to shrug off the dark scenarios flashing through my mind. The Master being here meant he'd crossed over and none of the others had stopped him. Which meant Selena, Anna, and Nicholas were either dead, or captured.

"You've already found the spirits here. Leaders of the guides from centuries ago. How many more do you think there are?" the Master said. "More than your friends can handle, at least."

"If you hurt them . . . " Katherine warned.

"You'll do what? I know you, spirit, and you don't have the skills to make me sweat."

"Maybe you haven't noticed that you're outnumbered," Graham said. "Three on one doesn't make for good odds."

"Do I look afraid?" the Master replied.

This was it. I could almost feel it, as though destiny were pulling us in to this one fight. One chance to get rid of the person behind the danger and death that had followed me for so long. Except I couldn't get Selena out of my head. I needed to know she was okay. Needed to make sure Selena, and Anna, and Nicholas weren't dead. Or about to be.

So I charged the Master, holding my sickle in one hand and Zolin's long staff in the other. Not an ideal combination, but this wasn't a time for perfection. The Master turned the sword, holding the blade straight behind him, and then stepped forward and swung it to meet my attack. As I closed, I planted the staff into the ground and pushed, jumped and swung my feet forward. I felt the sword swish beneath me, felt it take a part of my coat, as I kicked the Master in the chest.

I hit the ground, looked to see the Master picking himself up. I rolled forward and dove at him, tackling the man and bringing him to the floor with me.

"Go!" I said. "Save the others, and then come back for me."

Would my parents listen, or would they try to exact their own vengeance? Either way, I couldn't pay attention. The Master knocked my hands away and, somehow, lifted me up and threw me to the side. I caught myself on the wall, glancing towards the stair to see Katherine and Graham vanishing up it.

"It doesn't matter," the Master said, following my look. "They're running into a trap."

"What, that army of spirits you had before?"

"Those aren't any spirits, they're all guides. Or they used to be," the Master said. He picked his sword up off the ground and turned to face me. My sickle looked awfully small in comparison. "Many of them so old that they didn't even have weapons. Or the ones they used have broken over the ages, leaving them with nothing more than what they can scrounge."

"Why are they still here?" I asked.

Part of me wanted to attack straightaway. Part of me wanted to throw everything against the Master. The other part of me knew I held a small sickle and, with that sword, the master could cleave me in half without thinking about it. I had to hope that Graham and Katherine, that the others would come back and together we could overwhelm the Master. So I tried to keep him talking.

"A pact," the Master said. "One that is becoming unnecessary."

"A pact?"

The Master took another pair of steps and scraped the sword along the ground in an upward swing towards my torso. I back-stepped out of reach and danced along the edge of the platform, near the cliff with the Cycle spreading out behind me. The Master followed my moves, but with indifference.

He didn't want to kill me.

"As you now know, Carver, you can be the path out of Riven," the Master said. "A controlled valve to relieve the pressure in these dark times."

"You make it sound so simple." I slipped between the ever-flowing stream of spirits. If nothing else, the ghosts of people past would make good shields against any sword swings.

"It should be," the Master said. "If you cannot see what is happening, that Riven is collapsing, then you are more blind than I expected."

"So the only way to save Riven is to give you what you want?" I said. "That's convenient."

"Again I make the offer, and again you refuse," the Master said. "If you will not change your mind, then I will keep you here, trapped in Riven, until your sleeping body can be found."

"Try it," I said.

Instead of answering me, the Master turned towards the stream of spirits. I followed his eyes and, mixed with the common people and soldiers flooding down to the Cycle, moved a pair in medieval tunics. Strong and without will, they shuffled to the edge and jumped into the Cycle with the others.

"With every victory your friends earn," the Master said. "I grow stronger. With every broken binding, your hope dims. Now, Carver, I think it's time to shut that mouth of yours. The passage will open with your life, it does not require anything more."

The Master hefted the sword and swung, cleaving a line through the spirits and scattering their bodies across the ground. He stepped into the gap, his glare coming through his mask into my eyes. I backpedaled until I felt my foot brush the one thing that could get me out of this alive.

Chapter 32
Ugly Odds

As the Master ran forward I bent down, grabbed Takeda's katana, and thrust it like a spear. The Master slid to the side, brought his sword crashing down on the katana and battered it from my hand. Takeda's weapon flew away over the cliff and into the Cycle, joining its owner in the next life. But it had bought me a moment's momentum.

I lunged in with the sickle, tried to get inside the Master's reach. Leaving the great sword in his right hand, the Master met my strike with his left. Grabbed my wrist as the sickle closed in on his head and held it firm. I stared into that black rock mask, those eyes hidden under the dark of his hood, and tried to find some measure of humanity.

The Master tried to bring the great sword back, so I copied his move and gripped his right wrist with my left hand. We grappled, our strength measured in my desperation and his determination. I heard the Master gasp, not out of surprise, or fear, but of delight. His left hand twisted my wrist back, pushed the sickle away, and I used the push to back up from the Master and get out of the sword's range. Where the Master had found that sudden surge of strength, I didn't know.

"Another binding gone," the Master said. "Carver, save your friends. Stop this futility."

The Master let me get my distance, let me circle him and put my back to the spirits, to the path up the Mountain. Again the Master took his time, toying with me. I saw his gaze sweep back to the stair; another odd spirit amid the horde. Another one in older dress, but this one I recognized.

"Pierce," I said. The Master nodded. "He died 20 years ago?"

"I bound him on that day," the Master replied, following my retreat around the room.

"How? How could you manage to bind all of them?"

"So many questions," the Master said. "What does it matter?"

He hefted his sword again, and when he came towards me, I threw the sickle at his face and ran. I wouldn't win that fight. Not with a weapon I didn't know how to use, against an enemy stronger than me, and who seemed to have every advantage. I skipped up the stairs, pushing and knocking spirits down around me. Trying to create any obstacle I could to keep the Master from pursuing. Or at least to buy me some time.

I made it back up to the landing, where the Master's bed sat, and saw a slaughter. Graham and Katherine were working alongside Anna and Selena, with Nicholas watching, as they carved into a long line of spirits. Former guide leaders, most of them weaponless, all of them charging in with reckless abandon to be fought and wrangled by my friends.

The Master sacrificing his army for himself.

"They're bound to him," I called. "With every death you're making him stronger."

"Then what do you propose we do?" Graham said, smashing his hammer into the face of another elder spirit. "We have to fight, or they'll tear us apart."

"Then don't wrangle them," I said. "Keep the fire out."

Selena, her cleaver glowing, twisted her wrist as she bit in to the next spirit. The fire went out and, instead of falling to the ground blank-eyed and ready to be cycled, the spirit lurched away, grabbing at its injured throat. The spirit would recover, eventually, but it still took strength from the Master.

"Carver, behind you!" Anna called. I turned and saw the Master, sword high, hacking through spirits as he made his way up the stairs.

"Graham, Katherine. We have to take him together," I said. "Selena, Anna, you keep the other spirits back."

My parents heard the call and twisted away from their targets. Selena stepped in to cover as the three of us turned towards the Master. I reached for my belt, and realized I had no weapon. Graham glanced at me and laughed.

"Better leave this one to the two of us," Graham said. "You're only going to get in the way."

He wasn't wrong. I needed to find a weapon, and fast. I backpedaled away as Katherine and Graham engaged. They kept the Master pinned on the stairs; Graham's hammer forcing the Master to intercept with his great sword. Katherine tried to get behind, to batter the Master with her batons. As she moved, the Master back-stepped down the stairs and cut his great sword in a high arc to his left. The blade cut into Katherine's leg, knocking her down with a scream.

A spirit tackled me from behind. A crazy maniac with the beard longer than my torso. His hands clawed for my face and I batted them away. We rolled across the floor as I tried to get my elbow under the spirit's chin to force his snapping teeth away. We hit a rock wall, stopping our tumbled with me on my back. The spirit pressed his knee up into my stomach, twisting my intestines and sending my vision spinning. One of the spirit's hands reached back, elbow cocked and ready to deliver a fist into my eyes, when I saw a flash. Nicholas stabbed the spirit with one of the crossbow bolts he'd carried for me, back when we'd first left the apartment, when I still had the weapon.

The bolt burst into blue fire, wrangling the angry spirit. I pushed the idle body off of me, another soul restored to the Master.

"Thanks," I said to Nicholas, climbing to my feet. "Got any more of those?"

Nicholas shook his head. "I've already used several."

I turned back to the stairs and saw Graham mounting a frantic defense as the Master fought his way back up. He was swinging faster than he had before, the strikes more precise. Graham did everything he could to keep the hammer bouncing the sword away. The Master turned a cross swing into an overhead stab. Graham swung the hammer up from the ground, and deflected the blow, but the Master wheeled with the momentum, bringing the great sort back around faster than Graham could halt his own hammer swing.

The Master yelled, a bellow of pain. Katherine had clawed her batons into his legs. Lying there, grievously wounded, she delivered a strike that saved Graham's life, such as it was. Graham did not waste it. My father twisted his shoulders sent the hammer smashing into the Master's head. The blow struck the black crystal mask and shattered it, sent the Master staggering back down the steps.

I locked on his face. Clear in the blue light of the Cycle. The old eyes, the thick white beard, long gray hair of Piotr, living leader of the guides.

Chapter 33

A Forced Goodbye

I wanted to ask a thousand questions. A thousand things I wanted to say in that instant when I saw his face. When I saw that Piotr had been behind all of the attacks, the binding and suffering of my parents, and the threats to my friends. Before I could voice any of them, though, I heard Anna cry behind me.

"There's too many!" Anna sounded frantic and I turned. They were overwhelmed. Five spirits were driving Selena and Anna back, all of them bearing multiple wounds, strikes that should have wrangled the spirits. Instead, the cuts meant nothing to those already dead. Using the blue fire, though, would only make Piotr stronger.

I had to make a call. If we stayed and didn't finish Piotr in a minute, we'd be overwhelmed. If we left, assuming we made it out, who knew when we'd make it back here.

Behind me, Graham continued his desperate defense, Piotr's toothy smile growing with every swing. In front of me, Selena yelped as a spirit raked her forearm. We couldn't win.

"We have to run," I said. "Use the fire!"

Selena and Anna didn't hesitate, once more cloaking their weapons in blue flame and slashing their way through the spirits. I pushed Nicholas after them.

"Carver," I heard my father yell. "Get them out of here!"

"Working on it," I replied. Not that I was doing much. What I wouldn't have given for my lash. For those knives right now. Selena and Anna, they were doing work. Ducking underneath scratching nails and sidestepping shoulder charges to deliver stabs and jabs with scavenged weapons, sending one spirit after another to blue burning doom.

I followed Selena, Anna, and Nicholas up the stairs towards the exit. Glanced back to my parents, still holding Piotr on the stairwell. Piotr looked like he was playing, testing the reach of the hammer. My mother was on the floor, holding her injured leg. Unable to move. Unable to run.

"Keep going," I said the Nicholas and the others. "Keep running until you're outside and then keep running still."

"What are you doing?" Selena asked, turning back.

"I can't leave them," I said.

"I can help you."

"Protect Nicholas," I said. "He'll need you."

Selena nodded, then reached inside her coat and pulled out her long knife. It seemed pitifully small next to the great sword, but I counted one weapon better than none. So when she tossed it my way, I caught it and called my thanks.

"Remember Carver," Selena said. "We need you too."

I took the comment and started back down the steps. I didn't have any intention of dying here. I didn't plan to let my parents die either.

Back in the circle, Graham and Piotr engaged in a deadly dance. As I stepped into the clearing, I saw my mother make another move. Darting with her remaining baton, dragging her left leg, she lunged at Piotr's back. The strike a second slower than she used to be. Piotr caught the motion and continued his swing, turning with the blade back to catch my mother's baton.

Piotr's sword sliced through the baton, and if my mother hadn't fallen to the ground, he would've taken her apart too. Piotr whirled with the swing, shifting his feet and bringing the blade back up and over his head. Swung down towards Graham as my father's hammer slammed towards Piotr's chest. They struck each other, Graham's hammer crushing into Piotr's cloak as Piotr's sword cleaved into Graham's shoulder.

Graham's blow staggered Piotr and he went to one knee, leaning on the great sword. But only for second. Then Piotr rose back to his feet and towered over Graham, crippled on the ground. Piotr raised the sword, and Graham shot a wire from his wrist. It wrapped around Piotr's right hand, burst into flame, and Piotr stumbled back, trying to pull the wire off and shifting the sword to his left hand.

I went towards Katherine, reaching for her, but when she saw me my mother pulled away. "Get out of here, Carver," she said. "For once, let us save you."

I started to reply, but my mother stole the words from my mouth. She grabbed the broken half of her baton, and charged Piotr, still struggling with the wire. Swiped the clawed weapon at his face, and struck home. Opened a long gash along Piotr's cheek, but it wasn't enough. Piotr twisted his left wrist, sending blue fire streaming down the length of his sword. Even with only one hand, strengthened by the return of so many of his spirits to the Cycle, Piotr put an end to Katherine with a turning stab.

"Go," Graham said, pulling himself to his knees. "Don't let it be for nothing!"

I saw my father reach for the knife in his belt, and then I ran. I pushed through the spirits, shoved past the blank faces of the dead. I didn't stop to think about anything other than the next foot in front of me until I was out in the forest. Anna, Selena, and Nicholas were waiting, looking at me with hope that died as they met my eyes.

"It's over," I said. "Go back to the city."

We fled. I felt a part of me, the piece that I had given to Katherine, return as our binding broke. I heard Anna's gasp as Graham's borrowed soul came back to her. I'd lost the parents that I had barely known. Taken by an enemy that at last had a face. A name.

Piotr.

Chapter 34

Faults and Failures

When we reached the stump, Selena and Nicholas kept going. A long run back to the city. Anna and I, though, we had to cross back. I didn't know when we'd be able to catch up with the two spirits. We needed to find a bed that hadn't been used, or that could cross us back into Riven' city.

That could come later. Now I wanted to breathe. Find a drink and remember my parents. Nurse my growing anger.

We crossed back into the zeppelin. The windows of our room showed a spotted sky as the airship buzzed over one of the Great Lakes.

Maybe Michigan, or maybe we were farther. The sun setting, that Golden orb lighting the tops of the clouds in purple and orange fire.

"I'm so sorry," Anna said as she sat up.

"It's not your fault," I said, my voice flat.

"We could have done more. We let him come in. Cross over. There were so many spirits that we didn't notice."

"We didn't know," I said, standing up. "We couldn't have known that he'd bound all of them. That every single one we wrangled made him stronger."

Anna said nothing for a minute. I embraced that silence. We'd come so close. Had hit Piotr's base with numbers, at the right time. Only we didn't know what was inside, and Anna and I were missing our weapons. Whether that would have even made a difference. Graham had been one of the strongest fighters I'd ever seen, and my mother wasn't any slouch either.

Piotr had demolished both of them, barely getting hurt in the process. Going after him again would be suicide. So rather than think on it, I decided to solve a simpler problem.

"A drink?"

"Yes please." Anna picked up the wine, held it towards me. "There's this bottle right here."

I shook my head. "I need something harder."

We made our way to one of the dining areas, to a long metal counter with a sign overhead labeling it the *Sky Bar*. At various ends of the letters small fans turned through some mysterious power. Beneath the sign a pair of bartenders mixed up concoctions from a plethora of vices. A rotating menu declared specialties from where we were flying over at that moment in time. I asked for vodka. Anna ordered her gin. Both on the rocks.

Why did I feel so torn up? So shredded by the loss of two people who, less than a year ago, I didn't know existed? That I thought had abandoned me? Even when I found them, Graham and Katherine weren't alive. They couldn't come over for dinner, go on trips, or enjoy coffee on a cold morning. Our only bonding experiences had been frenetic fights for Riven's survival.

Yet I couldn't seem to summon words. Every sentence that came to my mouth died as the fight with Piotr replayed itself over and over and over again.

How many mistakes I'd made. How many opportunities I'd had to reverse things. Why hadn't I grabbed Selena's knife earlier? Why did I let the katana fall, or keep the sickle? A dozen other choices all turned wrong as I relived the moments.

"How do you deal with it?" I asked Anna. "With your parents?"

"This," Anna said, raising her glass. "And the memories. The times we laughed. The hopes and dreams we shared with each other. I cling to those."

"Wish I had those to turn to," I said.

"You do. How many times did you explore with them over the last few months? How many times did you get to do what you *live for* with the ones you loved? I'd say that's lucky, regardless of how it ended."

"Ghoul hunting as treasured family bonding time." I gave a short laugh.

"There's worse things," Anna said, her eyes stuck to the windows looking out over the water below.

I nodded and sipped more chilled liquor. The vodka felt good on my tongue, a warm nova in my stomach. I figured a trail of the drinks would eventually lead me back to the cabin, and to a hopefully dreamless sleep. When I woke up, I'd be . . .

"Where are we flying?" I said, realizing I had no idea of our destination.

"New York," Anna said. "Sorry if it's not where you want to go, but I figured we didn't have time to be picky."

"It's fine. We just have to figure out how to get back."

"What's your plan?" Anna replied. "We went in there with everything we had and lost. We're fugitives out here too. There are places we can hide, but not forever."

"I'm not going to hide. We have to take down Piotr."

"Maybe you didn't hear me," Anna said. "We tried that. It didn't work. Without Graham and Katherine, we'll be slaughtered."

"Only if we try the same thing."

"I'm listening."

"We hit him here. Outside of Riven. He won't have his sword, he won't have an army of spirits to help him."

"You're saying we try to murder the leader of the guides? I don't think that's going to work."

"Anna, it's either him or me. Or, worse, we keep dancing around each other until Riven breaks open and we all lose."

"Is stopping Piotr going to save Riven?" Anna asked.

"I don't know. But it can't hurt."

Chapter 35

Discovered

"Carver Reed," a familiar voice said as a hand clapped on my shoulder. "Didn't expect to see you on this ship."

I turned into the questioning face of Opperman, the newspaper reporter who seemed to always pop up at the strangest times. He wore more than his usual working coat. A level of finery and sophistication that I'd never seen Opperman adopt before, and he didn't look too comfortable in the outfit. A beggar sneaking into a play, or a nice restaurant.

"What are you doing here?" I asked.

"Flying to New York, same as you," Opperman said. "Say, how did you fare back there? Those couple of thugs get their hands on you?"

"Not yet." I glanced around, didn't see anyone watching us. "I'm trying to keep a low profile for that reason."

"Well then, you might want to try not looking like a guide," Opperman said. "Especially on a ship to New York for the peace summit."

"Peace summit?" Anna asked.

"Indeed. It starts tomorrow," Opperman said. "I'm covering for the newspaper. Everyone's going to be there."

"Everyone?" I said.

"Everyone that matters," Opperman said. "Even the leader of your own group, that Piotr fellow, is making a speech. You sure you're not going?"

I shook my head. "Just needed to get out of the city for a while."

I saw the change come over Opperman's face, the eyes turn from genial conversation to that hard-edged look the reporter had whenever he was hunting for a quote. The man had a nose for a story and once Opperman found the scent, he wouldn't be deterred.

"Mind giving me a clue why?" Opperman asked. "The guides having a fight? if Riven's in danger, then the world ought to know."

"It's nothing to do with the rest of the guides."

"Is he right?" Opperman asked Anna. "Also, forgive my manners, I don't believe we've met, Miss?"

"Smith," Anna said. " I think Carver's got the right opinion on this. Nothing to talk about."

Opperman sat back in his chair and appraised us. "So you're saying that the two of you, and by the look of it you're both guides, are on this ship and *not* going to the summit that literally everyone else on board is heading for?"

"A coincidence, really," I said.

"An unfortunate one, then." Opperman swung his head to the right. "Aren't those the two fellows that were trying to grab you in Ezra's?"

I followed his eyes and saw Polk and Derringer, sitting at the table across the room. They hadn't noticed us yet, which might have something to do with the fact that both were bandaged, sipping wine, and looking thoroughly the worse for their fight with Bryce.

"We didn't see them get on," I said.

"We went right into Riven," Anna said. "I don't know how long the ship stayed docked after we boarded."

"We've been in the air for some hours now. I should say we're somewhere over Ohio," Opperman said. "You say you crossed over? And did what? Anything I could file as a story?"

"Opperman, shut it," I said. "We need to get back to our cabin without those two knowing we're here."

"You'll need a distraction. I think I can provide one, for a story."

"If you can wait until after the summit is over I can give you one heck of a story," I said. "Above the fold, as you say."

"If you were anyone else I wouldn't take your word. But a reporter needs to protect his sources, and you, Carver, are one of my best."

I downed the rest of my vodka, and Anna shot her gin. I nodded for Opperman to commence whatever plan he had cooking. The reporter stood up from his chair and wandered over to the two guides. Took a seat at the table. Started talking. I watched their eyes as the two guides slowly recognized Opperman as the man who'd knocked them down back in Chicago, when Polk and Derringer had first tried to arrest me. I could see them glazing over at Opperman's barrage of questions.

"Time to make a move," I said. "You go first. They don't know you as well."

Anna nodded, slipped out of the chair and made her way through the dining room. She crossed through the crowd and, as I walked, neither Polk nor Derringer looked up at her. One down, me to go. I shrugged out of my coat and held the heavy thing in my arms. Underneath I only had a plain white shirt, a tad less distinctive than the guide coat.

In front of me were tables and chairs, people mixing in and out as they decided on afternoon meals, cocktails, or more. Polk and Derringer were on the left side, so I veered right. Went around one table. Scooted behind a large gentleman who seemed intent on eating an entire cow by himself. A waiter in front of me handed out champagne to everybody around a larger table. I slipped behind her and kept moving. Almost clear.

I heard a rattle behind me, a tinkle of glass as someone's flute whacked against the tabletop and shattered. Someone yelped and I turned, against my own judgment, to see what was going on. The large man with the steak was beating on his own chest, his face turning purple. A couple of waiters ran over, one was trying to dislodge whatever chunk of meat had found itself trapped within his throat. All eyes went to the struggle. Then I felt a pair on me.

I looked to my right and saw Polk and Derringer, their eyes dead set on mine.

I ran.

Chapter 36

Emergency Action

We dashed through the airship and into our cabin. As the door shut, I looked back in the hallway and didn't see either of the two guides there. We'd either lost Polk and Derringer, or they'd taken too long to get up from the table. If we were lucky, Anna and I would be able to hide in our room.

"Until we land, anyway," Anna said to my remark. "There's not exactly other ways off the ship."

"When we're on the ground, I feel like we can find another way out," I said. "In the meantime, we'll just have to be careful. "

"You mean starve?" Anna said. "Stay in this room for the next day?"

"Did you think the fugitive life was a glamorous one?"

"For a second I dared to hope," Anna said, sitting down on the bed. "Did you hear what Opperman said?"

"Piotr's going to be in New York. We'll have a chance."

Anna opened her mouth to reply when a crackling noise came from the hallway. A gravelly, distorted voice spoke.

"This is your captain. We've been informed that there are a pair of potential criminals on board our aircraft," the voice said over an intercom. "In order to ensure the safety of our crew, and our passengers, I'm ordering everyone to return to their cabins until further notice. We will be conducting a cabin by cabin search until the suspects are found and apprehended. We apologize for the inconvenience, and hope you understand that the safety of our guests is paramount."

Not good. A cabin by cabin search? I looked around our room, confirmed there were not, in fact, a bevy of hiding places. Squeezing beneath the beds seemed like a poor choice.

"So do we wait?" Anna asked. "We could stand by the door, ambush them when they open it?"

"We can't fight all of the guards on the ship. This isn't Riven. We don't have our weapons."

Which meant we'd have to try another way. Staying in the cabin was a nonstarter, but the mass thumping going on outside, feet pounding on the hallways above and below us as people scurried to their cabins . . . that meant opportunity.

"They won't search the crew area," I said. "If we can hide there, we might stand a chance."

"It's as good a plan as any."

I opened our cabin door and looked into the hallway. People running back and forth, yammering at their spouses and friends. Ducking into cabins and slamming shut the doors. I threw my coat on and we left. Took a right turn and headed away from the dining area and the bar, towards the ship's engines.

A stairwell at the end of the hall led up and down, next to it stood a door marked, in bold white letters: NO ADMISSION—CREW ONLY. I turned the knob and found it locked. Anna pounded on the door before I could suggest trying another route. A moment later the knob turned and the door opened, an irritated serviceman already talking on the other side.

"Did you lose your key again?" the serviceman said before realizing we were not, in fact, part of his crew. I pushed him back through the doorway, clapping my hand over his mouth. Anna slipped in behind me and shut the door. I pressed the crewmen up against the wall, a narrow one lacking the finery of the passenger quarters. Further along I could see the hall split into a series of catwalks and compartments, space for churning engines, mechanical parts, crew bunks, and bathrooms.

"You're going to take us to the engines," I said to the serviceman.

"The engines?" Anna asked.

"We can't hide here for another day until the ship reaches New York," I said. "We need to bring her down, now."

The serviceman, eyes wide, tried to nod. I didn't move my hand. Not giving the guy a chance to scream.

"Now, we're a pair of guides that you're leading on a ship inspection," I said to the serviceman. "That's what you're going to tell anyone we run into. Don't try anything, or I'll snap your neck. Then I'll cross over to Riven, find your spirit there, and make sure you go straight to the Cycle."

The serviceman tried to nod again, more frantic than before. I let my hand fall away and he sucked in a large breath. My left hand balled into a fist, ready to sock him in the kidneys if he tried to shout. Guess the serviceman didn't want to risk his life for no reason, as he stepped away and waved us down the hall.

"Follow me," the serviceman said loudly. "If you want to see the engines and make sure they're safe, I'll take you right to them."

"We're turning into real criminals," Anna whispered to me. "First evading arrest, now taking a hostage?"

"You can always say I pressured you into it," I said. "Threatened you, blackmail, take your pick."

"What about you?"

"I don't know," I replied. "I'll figure something out."

The serviceman led us past the bunks in the bathrooms, through a series of black metal catwalks bordered by gaskets blowing steam, shifting and churning pistons, and a maze of pipes. Copper lights hung from the ceiling by threads of wire, their yellowed glow giving a rich bronze cast to the world. Apparently most of the crew members were helping with the search, because the back rooms were deserted. Only a skeleton set making sure things were running well.

Valves covered the engine room. Large and small wheels controlling the pressure and fuel leading to various fans keeping the zeppelin aloft. A woman stood there working them in a pressed royal blue uniform. She turned as the serviceman entered and regarded us with the baleful stare of someone interrupted out of deep concentration.

"Now is not the time," the woman said. "We're executing an altitude change to get through a rough patch."

"They wanted to talk to you, Wynn," the serviceman said.

"We need you to bring the ship down," I said, cutting right to it. "The criminals on board are dangerous. They could disable the vessel. We don't want fatalities."

Wynn stared at me, then moved her eyes to the serviceman, then to Anna. "Who are you?" Wynn asked.

"I'm a guide," I said. "We're trying to catch a pair of fugitives."

"Right," Wynn said. "The only person who can tell me to bring the ship down is the captain. You want to change this flight, you talk to him."

We didn't have time for that. Not to mention that the odds of us getting all the way back out of this area and to the bridge without running into problems were zero. Time to cross another line.

"Wynn, let's make this real simple," I said. "The world is at risk. We're the only ones who can save it. In order to do that, this ship needs to be on the ground, now."

Wynn raised her eyebrow. "I already told you. The ship stays up unless the captain tells me otherwise."

Anna pushed past me, walked right up to Wynn and pressed her into the valves behind her. "Listen, Wynn. He's telling the truth. We're not above doing what we need to do to get what we want. Either you take the ship down now, or we play a game where I see how many of these valves I have to twist to send the ship into a dive. Which do you think gives you a better chance to live?"

Wynn shifted her eyes between the two of us. "I'll do it."

Anna turned back to me. "See? You're not the only one who can talk tough."

I barely saw the move, the change in Wynn's expression as she shot an elbow into Anna's side. The mechanic reached up and slapped a button next to the valves, one labeled emergency assist. Overhead alarms rang.

And to think, for a second I'd thought we might actually pull this off.

Chapter 37

Bring it Down

The serviceman decided to be a hero and came at me as Anna and Wynn struggled by the valves. He punched like a man who had never fought before, wide and slow, afraid of hitting his target. I ducked the swing and swept my leg through his, tripping him to the ground. I glanced behind us, to the hallway where we'd come in from, and hoped to find a door. Nothing. Any reinforcements would have easy access.

I heard a yell, and turned back to find Wynn on the floor. Anna went to the valves and started twisting the wheels. Shutting them at random.

"I don't think—" I started.

"You're going to bring it down and kill us all," Wynn said from the ground, then pushed herself off of the floor and jumped into a low tackle.

I felt the serviceman grabbing at my ankles and stepped away, raised my foot and threatened to stamp on his face. The serviceman caught the gesture and held up his hands. Why risk yourself when reinforcements had to be on the way?

The airship lurched as the whole world tilted on its axis and sent us falling to the right. My shoulder rammed into the room's side wall, the metal pipes providing nothing in the way of cushioning. I heard shouts from up the hall. Crew members having a hard time keeping their own footing as the ship twisted and turned.

Anna kept herself upright, hands gripping a pair of valves while Wynn held onto Anna's coat. Trying to pull herself forward.

"Then tell me how to land," Anna yelled to the mechanic.

"You can't do it all from here," Wynn replied. "It takes a captain to steer."

Anna reached up and dialed another valve to the right, sealing it. "He'll get the idea."

"You're insane," Wynn said.

"We're desperate," I countered.

My stomach climbed up my throat as the ship entered a steeper drop. Fans were shutting off as the listing craft accelerated towards the ground. Towards a very messy landing.

"Fine!" Wynn said. "Reopen the one on your right. After five seconds open the one on your left. They'll equalize."

Anna did that, twisted the valves open. Gradually I felt the ship start to pull up out of its suicide dive. My ability to stand came back and I pushed myself off the wall. Just in time for the serviceman to come at me again.

He opted for the less precise method of the shoulder charge, running right in at my chest. The serviceman pinned me back against the wall as I wrapped my arm around his neck, slung my left foot behind his ankles and once more slammed the man to the ground. This time I didn't let up. Gave him a vicious kick; the man going limp. I'd never knocked someone out here before. Only in Riven. More lines being crossed, and all because of Piotr.

Wynn pushed Anna to the side, using the ship's momentum and Anna's larger coat to drag my friend away from the valves and throw her to the floor. I moved to help, then paused as two more servicemen ran into the room, these brandishing stun batons. Two on one, and I had no weapon. So I did the only thing I could.

I ran for the valves. Crossed the room as the servicemen started after me. I spun as many valves as I could to the right. Wynn tried to stop me, but Anna reversed their positions, clinging to Wynn's back and forcing her to her knees. An ugly fight.

The airship lurched again. I heard the servicemen yell as they were driven back in the wall. I copied Anna's technique; kept my hands on the valves. I felt as though I were hanging from a cliff, the valves my only handholds.

"You have to open some or you'll kill us all," Wynn pleaded.

"Not until there's no other choice," I said. "This ship's landing."

There weren't any windows in the engine room, no way of telling how close to the surface we were. Adrenaline and nausea shot through me, my stomach flipping end over end. I didn't fear dying, really—so far as deaths went, going out in an airship crash seemed to be one of the better ones. Only, I didn't want to kill all the others on the flight. The other passengers had no idea they'd boarded the wrong ship. Piotr's catastrophe shouldn't hurt them too.

"Tell me when," I said to Wynn.

"Now," Wynn said. "Do it now. At least two of them."

Wynn might've been lying. I couldn't tell. Like she'd played Anna. If the ship would right itself and we'd be captured. If Wynn had told the truth, though, and I did nothing, everyone would die. So I turned the valves. Opened them and felt the fans churn as the airship struggled to pull itself upright.

Other alarms added to the cacophony. I didn't know what the noises meant, but I assumed I was doing something right. An assumption that proved true a moment later with the first loud crack from somewhere up front. Followed by another and another. A section of the hallway ripped away in a brief flash of a brown tree trunk, pine needles scattering everywhere. Branches tore through.

We were going down into a forest.

"Hold on!" I yelled to nobody and everybody. Because I couldn't think of anything else to say. Because everything in front of us vanished into a massive green, brown, crackling terror. I kept my grip on the valves, ducked my head into my chest and tried to survive.

Chapter 38

On Foot

Sunflowers grew everywhere. Yellow, brown, and tall. I saw them outside of the ship, I saw them within a few feet of me as I pried my fingers loose from the valves and took a fleeting step forward. We had crashed through a forest and, somehow, the captain had put us down in a wide field. The walkways in front of us had been torn away entirely. Wreckage scattered all around, but the engine room held. The thick pipes providing shelter.

Around me the servicemen groaned. Wynn looked unconscious, and I pulled her away to see Anna trapped against the wall. Her eyes closed and a gash marring her forehead.

Probably where Wynn had fallen into her. I picked Anna up, hefted her in her coat. Stood on my aching knees and walked away from the ship.

I ducked under bars and beams, the occasional burst of steam spraying hot wet air over my face. Pieces of torn canvas whirled in the wind, slapping around like the wings of an enormous bird. Shouts for help and rescue rang out as people realized they weren't dead. I kept walking. Crunching over the plants and getting out from beneath the vessel.

The field was huge. Stretching for hundreds of yards. Every inch of it covered in tall sunflower stalks. I tried to shield Anna from their leaves, kept her face covered by her coat. Warm summer sunlight blazed at us, super-heating me, causing sweat to run out of every pore. I didn't know where we'd landed, but staying by that ship and getting captured would make the disaster worthless.

Eventually we reached the forest at the edge of the field and there, underneath the shade of the trees, I risked a look back. The airship looked like a beached whale, its great bulk sliding slowly to the ground as the zeppelin deflated. I could still hear cries, and saw at least one or two riders on horseback had come galloping up to the vessel. Help would be coming. Those who could be saved, would be saved. I hoped Opperman was among them.

"You thought I was reckless before, Selena," I muttered to myself. "Wait till you hear about this."

We went for another hour through the woods, walking over pine needles and taking in the smells of ferns and blooming flowers. Chirping birds and the scuffles of animals in the deep. Anna dragged on my arms, a consequence of time more than weight. Our coats—I'd taken off mine—had to be tucked with us. I made frequent breaks and pauses to catch my breath. Stops to make sure Anna still breathed.

"Carver?" Anna spoke up as I trudged along, the day sinking deeper into the afternoon. "Where are we?"

"I have no idea. But we're alive."

"My head hurts.".

"You've got a nasty cut," I replied. "I'm hoping we can find somewhere to set you down soon, because my arms are going to give out."

"Oh. I think I can walk."

"That would be lovely."

I helped her to stand, and Anna immediately fell against me. Her legs had power, she could move, she just needed support. So we kept walking as afternoon dwindled into evening and the sun fell behind the horizon. I did not want to be stuck in the forest all night. We didn't have any camping gear, no food or water, and Anna needed treatment for her cut.

"Over there," Anna said, pointing. "Do you see it?"

A small town flickered in the twilight, peeking between tree trunks and low, leafy branches. I'd been looking for salvation the entire time, but now that we'd potentially found it, I hesitated. A farmhouse maybe, someplace where odds of us running into other survivors were slim. A town only a few hours walk away from a crash? We wouldn't be the only ones heading there.

"Carver," Anna said at my hesitation. "I don't think I can keep going."

"Then let's get you some help," I said, and we turned towards those burning lights. Being free wouldn't help us if Anna died, or if her gash became infected.

The town grew. As we came closer and left the forest, I realized the dense tree trunks blocked much of the town from view. Traffic; motorcars and horses and a rail line, washed their noise over us as we approached. We didn't have a good way to cover Anna's gash, something that would draw commentary if seen, so as we came close Anna found a bench on the side of the road. Kept her head low and her hair covering the wound.

I continued into the town, trying to find some form of first-aid. A place we could stay that wouldn't ask questions. And hoped our crimes hadn't beaten us here.

Chapter 39

Slice of Life

A broad avenue, caught between old and new, cut through the center of town. Between motorcars and horses sharing the street, kicking up dirt and mud as they went by to the scattered flickers of neon signs going up outside storefronts and saloons, I realized that Chicago's common luxuries hadn't spread everywhere. No automated taxis, a lack of paved roads, and, on the other side of things, clean air.

My mask hung inside my coat, in the breast pocket designed to carry it. First there'd been Inman's camp, and now this town. I resolved to get out more. Find more places where the world wasn't best experienced through a filter.

I scanned the windows and the marquees, trying to find something that indicated a doctor. Some sort of a hospital or clinic. I passed by places selling food, drink, and virtually everything else a person might need. A small clock adorned every light post, their hands adding a mechanical cadence to the buzz of the place. People shuffled about without Chicago's hurried, frantic nature. Their eyes fell on my coat and didn't slide away but lingered, instead, with the curious fascination of seeing a legend come to life.

I made it a block and a half in before I saw the glowing heart hanging in a front window. Inside, through the glass, I saw the usual white coats of nurses and doctors tending to a smattering of patients covering the range from early evening drunk to late afternoon farm accident. A perfect spot.

I smuggled Anna to the place, keeping her head down and pressed into my chest, as though she were suffering from some sort of grief or cold, even though she wore her coat and the night was warm. Whatever attention we attracted quickly drew away to the roaring sound of another engine, the laughter echoing from a nearby bar, or even just a glance up at the starlit sky.

Out with Inman, that night in the bluffs, was my first time really seeing the glittering canopy that hung above us every night, that Chicago's endless glow made invisible. The town split the difference, its lights washing out the smaller stars but letting the brighter ones poke through. Part of me wondered if Riven lived on one of those, a place hung up somewhere in the cosmos that we happened to travel to when we crossed over.

Inside the clinic, a nurse took one look at Anna and leapt into action. Set her down on a chair, swabbed the wound with a wet towel, and set about to stitching it closed. Anna took the whole thing without talking, staring forward with a glazed look in her eye. Exhausted. Like me.

"Where did she get this?" a doctor asked me, stepping up to watch as the nurse finished closing the wound.

"Running through the woods," I said. "Tripped and fell."

"Aren't you a little old for those kinds of games?"

"Apparently not."

"It's none of my business," the doctor said. "But you two appear to be guides, correct?"

I said nothing for a moment. Weighed the answer. With the coats we were wearing, however, it would be obvious. I nodded.

"We're leaving town as soon as she's ready to go," I said.

"Look at her," the doctor replied. "Look at you, for that matter. You're in no state to go anywhere. Let me recommend you a hotel, nice and discreet."

"Why? What do you want?"

"I want nothing," the doctor said. "I have a daughter. Her name is Ada, and she is one of you. Lives east of here, in Pittsburgh. Is it true what they say, what I've been hearing, that it's getting worse over there? On the other side?"

"It is," I said. "War, disease, they hurt as much over there as they do here."

"I know you probably think those of us here don't care," the doctor said. "That we don't understand what you're doing. It's not true. We just don't know how to help."

"This helps," I said, gesturing it Anna. "Giving us places to sleep. Food and water. Those help."

"Then we will do what we can," the doctor said. "When she's done, the two of you can leave. No payment necessary."

I looked at Anna's face, her sagging eyes as the nurse cleaned up the stitches. "You mentioned a hotel?"

"It's a block further in," the doctor said. "Called *Pine's Rest*. Tell them we sent you and they'll treat you well. Remember that she has to get those out in a few days."

Minutes later the two of us were walking down the street towards the hotel. Anna kept her eyes crawling over the scenery. I tried to keep her standing straight.

"What were you talking about with the doctor?" Anna asked.

"For once, someone was saying thank you," I said.

"I bet that's a rare thing for you," Anna replied.

"I liked it better when you were quiet."

The *Pine's Rest* stood five stories of ordinary. Without the doctor's direction, I would have kept walking by. *Pine's Rest* had a small sign and dim windows, a lack of energy. Then again, we didn't want attention. I definitely didn't want excitement. For that, the *Pine's Rest* fit perfectly. We booked a room on a promise of paying in the morning and went upstairs. A pair of twin beds in a small space that made me reminisce about the airship's comforts.

I didn't have much money left on me and I didn't think Anna did either. If we were going to book passage all the way to New York, then the *Pine's Rest* would have to go without. Another crime to add to our growing list. A part of me despaired at how easily I came to that conclusion. Such small time acts no longer seemed to have relevance in a world growing darker and more desperate.

"I'm going to cross over," I said.

"I don't think I can," Anna said. "Not tonight."

"You could feel better on the other side?"

"Carver, haven't you had enough adventure for one day?"

"In this world, yes."

When I lied on the bed, the thriving hum on the street outside the window pouring in, I felt the pull towards sleep. That threat of diving deep into that unconscious pool. Rather than follow that pull, though, I focused my mind on Riven and attempted to cross.

Chapter 40
Where to Go

I lucked out. A guide had never used the bed before. It had no anchor in Riven, and so when I focused on the apartment I shared with Selena and Nicholas, I woke up right where I wanted to be.

Selena stood outside on the balcony, leaning over the edge and staring out over the city. As though nothing had changed.

"You made it back," I said.

"We ran the entire way," Selena replied. "I never realized how different we are over here. We never tired, Carver. I never had to stop and catch my breath. Never felt my legs give out. I ran right up to the door."

"Not everything about being a spirit is a disadvantage."

"I kept expecting it to happen. It was scary when it didn't. When my legs kept moving," Selena said, then glanced at me with a worried glint to her eye. "Look at me. Here I am talking about not getting tired, when you must be exhausted."

I told her the story. Bringing down the zeppelin and running through the forest while carrying Anna in my arms. Selena took the whole thing while barely batting an eye. At the end she nodded her head, gave me a sad smile.

"It seems like our lives are one mess after another," Selena said. "I'm glad you made it."

"I wouldn't mind a bit more calm." I reached out and took her hand. I'd never quite become used to how a spirit's touch felt in Riven, that lukewarm, almost placid feel. The lack of real blood moving through their veins. But I held on, threading my fingers through hers.

"So what are we doing now? I don't think we can attack the Mountain again."

"I agree," I said. "As much as I'd like to think we can beat him, Piotr's too strong. Anna and I are on our way to find him on the other side, where he won't have his weapons. His spirits. If we take him out over there, that will break his bindings. Piotr might even go right to the Cycle by himself."

"You really think that'll work?"

I shrugged. "It's all we've got."

We stood in silence for a minute, watching the sparks flare. Then Selena let go of my hand and pulled me in for a tighter hug.

"I'm sorry you never got to say goodbye to them," Selena said. "If it matters, Katherine and Graham were wonderful during the trip out. Were amazing to get to know while we stayed here in this apartment. They were always funny, always enjoying every moment together. Whether they were fighting spirits or not."

A side of my parents that I never saw. Yes, we had a chance over the last couple of months, after freeing Graham, to catch up with each other, but most of our nights had been spent chasing ghouls and closing breaches. Wrangling spirits to keep Riven whole. Not a lot of opportunity for family togetherness. Not a lot of opportunity to grow bonds between mother and father and son.

"Tell me more," I said. "Did you ever talk about their past? Who they were or what they wanted to be?"

Selena paused. Then spoke slowly. "Carver, you may not understand, but it feels strange to talk about life when you're no longer living. I don't talk about my children, or ask you to try to find them, because it feels like that part of me is no longer here. Katherine and Graham were the same. We only talked about what they'd done in Riven. Their adventures together."

"Never once?" I asked. "My mom never talked about how she died? Or what brought her and Graham together?"

Selena shook her head. "I'm sorry. Maybe we weren't close enough."

We stayed out there for a while longer. Talking, touching, and reveling in a moment without horror and violence. Sometimes I needed a reminder that those moments could actually happen in Riven, or outside of it.

"I'm going to go back to her house," I said. "I bet her diaries are still there. I never finished reading them."

"I'll go with you," Selena said. "There's no reason to stay here. Also, Nicholas is hard at work at something new."

"Something new?"

"You'll have to ask him. You remember him talking about the Cycle, how he wanted to learn more about it? I guess seeing how it worked in the Mountain gave him an idea."

We went downstairs to the bottom level, on the ground floor, and found Nicholas bent over a table. A lot of the machines that have been in the room had disappeared. When I asked the scientist he gestured towards the mound of metal and tubing and other scraps gathered together on that table.

"Riven isn't booming with raw material," Nicholas said. "So I'm converting it. I think the end result will be well worth it, however."

"What's that result going to be?" I asked.

"I'll know it when I find it," Nicholas said. "Right now it is only an idea. Something that might solve all of our problems if it turns out to be true. Or, if it's not the case, then I'll have merely wasted days and days of effort."

"Is that all?"

"Your tone implies that perhaps engaging in such random activities is, in fact, a waste of time," Nicholas replied. "I can assure you that it is not. Especially when time has no endpoint, provided you stay alive."

"Whether I live or die isn't looking too certain right now," I said.

"Don't take too long," Selena chimed in. "You know how we like your toys, Nicholas,"

"Toys?" Nicholas said. "Katherine and Graham never called them toys. I suppose it is too much to ask that I get some appreciation."

"We love you Nicholas," I said.

"If you really loved me, when you get back from wherever you're going, if you could bring another bit of metal. Any metal really, but I would prefer something thick. Iron or steel. If you would be so kind," the scientist said.

"We'll keep our eyes open."

Metal in Riven? Rare even if you weren't specifying a type. Where we were going? The Shambles? We'd be lucky if we found anything usable.

I wasn't going there for the scientist or his experiments. I was going there because, while Anna recovered, I wanted to find out what it really happened to my mother.

Chapter 41

A Mother's Words

Spirits always crowded the Shambles. The derelict buildings and broad streets providing ample room for the horde of spirits to run through on the way to the Cycle. More now than before. Less defined. The soldiers that used to make up so many of the dead running through here had thinned out, replaced by old and young. The diseased.

The word continued to be that the plague was spreading. More and more people suffering from what they called the flu. Selena and I moved among them, using the spirits for cover as we made our way through the district. Dodging guides along the way.

My mother's house stood open, the back door ajar as we left it those months ago when I found Selena there, a captive of Katherine's when Graham and, by extension, Piotr had bound her. Upstairs sat a series of tables stacked with pages covered in my mother's handwriting. I wanted to dive into those journals. To explore my own past.

Selena went to the far side and broke into the pages. I didn't have a specific goal, except to try to find out more about what had led my parents together. What had led to my mother dying shortly after my birth. To get there I shuffled through page after page of notes, discussions on various hunts Katherine had gone on with Bryce. Wondering paragraphs asking what I'd been doing. Feedback from Bryce on where I'd been moved to and who I lived with.

I'm not sure what I expected to find in the pages, what I thought would be revealed to me about my mother. I found that the life of a spirit in Riven shared many of the same problems I had on the other side. Boredom, a desire for purpose, and dreams were all there. Thoughts of choices not made haunted my mother's days. Joyful anecdotes about finding fascinating buildings, or meeting a spirit that hadn't yet gone astray and delving into a conversation. If anyone could say they had lived after dying, my mother had done so.

"Carver," Selena said. "I think I found what you wanted."

I went over and reached for the the first page that Selena was holding, but she moved it back.

"It's not easy reading," Selena said. "I can just tell you what it says?"

"I have to know," I said. "My mother said Piotr killed her. I need to know how, why."

Selena handed me the page without another word. Slid the next few beneath it. A stack of entries. I started to read:

I feel as though I'm starting to lose more of these memories. The things that have led me to this place, and who I am. As though my grasp on reality is fading. So I'm writing them down.

This memory starts in the spring of 1889. On a raid to close a breach. Some skirmish on the other side of the world that brought a lot of hapless soldiers into Riven at once. As happens when countries forget that their wars don't just affect the living. Graham wielded that hammer of his, a ridiculous weapon. One that gave him such a small window of flexibility. I remember laughing at it, saving him from a group of spirits that made their way inside his reach.

Rather than being haughty, or dismissive, Graham chose to play game with me. Challenged me to ever-increasing feats of stupidity here in Riven. Like anyone, I enjoyed pushing myself to the limits, so I didn't refuse. Together we soon were going on nightly adventures. Drawing closer and closer to each other. Until, six months later, Graham told me he was dying.

Told me that, on the other side, he had a disease that was eating away at his heart. I had never seen him over there. In Riven only. He lived on the West Coast, and I in Chicago. What point was there in journeying across the country to find each other when we could do so every night?

He made me promise. Promise to bind him when he died. When he felt he was going, Graham crossed over and stood with me next to him. I held his hand and he told me when he felt the cord binding him to his body sever. I replaced it with my own.

The next few pages talked about how they continued in Riven. How their love grew despite having no connection on the outside world. My mother started spending more time in Riven, often crossing back only to wake up, eat, take care of bodily needs, and then dive back in. At least until that fall.

I could feel it. Though I didn't know how. I was pregnant. With child. I didn't believe it at first, but I found myself having to cross back more often. Sickness presented itself at regular intervals. I was often tired. Graham promised to keep filling my quota while I was otherwise occupied. Because he was not present in my world, that was all he could do.

I scoured the libraries during the days. Spoke to other guides I felt I could trust. Even told Bryce, the new guide that I was mentoring at the time. Throughout history there had been a number of these children, born of spirits and people mingling in ways that, perhaps, were not intended. Most went on to lead the same lives that I or Graham or Bryce might live. Some, however, became targets.

As the summer wore on and my due date grew closer I noticed more attention paid to my activities. Guides not assigned to Chicago moved to the area, claiming they were visiting for other reasons. Neighbors I'd never spoken to noticed me in the halls. Asked me when I was due.

It wasn't long before I began to see them at night, before I crossed over. In the shadows during the day. I could feel them outside my apartment door. Waiting. I knew why. They wanted to take my child and use him, use him to bring the worlds together.

I secured Dr. Farth's promise that no one besides the medical staff would be allowed to enter during my labor. That no one would have access to my child beyond those required to keep him alive. But Dr. Farth had allegiances beyond my own. He had just been given the assignment to care for us, the guides in Chicago. He would not give it up for me.

It was on the night after Carver had left my arms to go away with the nurses that the first of the attempts was made. I do not know what was used, only that it was slipped inside my food, and when I refused that, my drink. I hid in Riven, replacing my weak body with my strong Riven half. Until eventually I too felt that cord slip away. That last tie to the world and my son.

Bryce bound me eventually, but Graham had disappeared. The price of our brief romance was my life, and, I could only imagine, that of my son.

Chapter 42

Allies Again

I put the last sheet down and stared out the windows into Riven's gray. I had it now. The history that led to me. The suspicion and fear that consumed my mother in her last days as she felt Piotr's thugs closing in. She'd known my condition, and accepted that Piotr would kill her for it.

The most terrible part, though, was that Katherine didn't feel like she could even try to stop it. At least not over there, in the real world where she lived alone. In Riven she had a chance; with her weapons and her friends. How strange that Riven, her salvation, had become more dangerous to me than the world she left behind?

"Carver," Selena said, moving over near the stairs. "I don't think we're alone."

I moved my hand to the lash. We had grabbed my equipment from Anna's place in the Warrens on our way over here. It felt good not to be relying on random weapons, but instead on the familiar gear that I'd worked with for so many years. Selena drew her cleaver and the two of us took up position, me looking over the stairs from behind and Selena ready to spring if the intruder made it to the top.

The stairs creaked as someone walked up. The moment any heads appeared, Selena would be able to take it off or I would be able to loop the lash around their neck.

But when I saw Alec's face, I hesitated.

"Don't kill me," Alec said. "I'm not here to fight."

"What if I don't believe you?" I said.

"This isn't about us. This isn't about you," Alec said. "They're going to cleanse Bryce."

Cleansing. Blinding was the usual punishment, a severing from Riven. A cleansing amounted to the capital degree. Taking your soul in Riven and sending it into the Cycle. Wiping you out in both this world and the other. Reserved only for the most severe offenders. I'd never heard of one ever being sentenced. More of a cautionary punishment than something actually delivered.

"Why?" I said.

"Because he helped you."

"That's ridiculous. Why aren't they just blinding him?"

"Piotr wants to make a statement," Alec said. "He says that the guides cannot be divided at this time. That we must all be together. However, cleansing Bryce is not the way."

"That's not the only problem with Piotr," I said. I brought Alec up to speed with the details. Who the Master really was. What happened to my parents. At the end of it, Alec reached out and shook my hand, then pulled me into a hug.

"I am sorry for what I have done," Alec said. "Will you forgive me?"

"Just this once," I said. "Next time, maybe give me a little more credit? Besides, I feel like knowing you never caught me is punishment enough."

"It will haunt me for the rest of my days, no doubt." Alec looked over at the stairs. "We have to hurry. They are already taking Bryce to the Cycle."

"One question," Selena said. "How did you find us here?"

"Easy," Alec said. "I knew Carver could never leave you. So I watched your apartment until he appeared. Love always makes for easy prey."

"You're so creepy."

"And you, *mon frier*, a spirit with a cleaver, are not?" Alec replied. Selena glanced at the blade in her hand and shrugged.

"Glad we could agree," I said, nodding towards the stairs. "They're taking Bryce? Let's go save him."

As we walked down the stairs and outside the house, Alec pointed to an object leaning against the entry wall. My crossbow.

"I thought, maybe, you would like it back," Alec said. "I found it beneath the beds. Hidden like a child's toy."

"Alec, I think this is the first gift you've ever given me," I said, refusing to acknowledge his judgment of my chosen hiding place.

"I recall giving you your life more than a few times," Alec replied.

I couldn't argue with that one.

Chapter 43

Stay of
Execution

Four guides, with Bryce in the middle. They were nearing the gate to leave the city through the Shambles, the stream of spirits making their way around and giving the guides plenty of room. Bryce, for his part, walked with his head up and his eyes gazing forward. Hands tied behind his back with a length of chain. Seeing my mentor a prisoner filled me with deep anger at ruined justice. This wasn't right, and Bryce walked in irons because of me.

"We're outnumbered by one," I said. "I'll take a shot with the crossbow, try to even it out. Selena, you get Bryce out of there. Alec and I will handle the other three."

"I can fight too," Selena said. "You don't have to protect me."

"He's not," Alec said. "Bryce is the most important target, and we don't want to kill the guides."

"If you can get Bryce away, then we can leave," I said and Selena nodded. Looked like she understood why I didn't want her carving up my former teammates.

We were in the bottom floor of a building a block behind the guides, a block of dry road and damned spirits marching out of the city. I went up to the second floor, climbing a stair that wobbled with every footfall. Riven's rot claiming the house piece by piece. Crept out onto an overhang, praying that it would hold my weight. It creaked and I heard something snap beneath me, but it stayed up. I lay down and set the crossbow in front of me, looked down the length of its shaft, and set my sights on the rear guide.

I loaded the normal bolt. Not enough, hopefully, to kill. Only incapacitate. As the front guide started underneath the open gate, I fired.

Pulled the trigger and, without waiting to see whether the bolt hit, dropped off the overhang and hit the street running.

Alec and Selena were out in front of me. Dashing along the side of the streets to stay out of the spirit crowd and sprinting towards the quartet of guides. Or, I should say, a trio. My shot had found its mark. The rear guide stumbled away from the rest, clutching at his back. The other three were losing their chance to get ready, looking at their companion and not paying attention to their approaching adversaries. Which was exactly the point.

Alec, gauntlets ready to work, sprang out from behind a pair of spirits and tackled the guide on the left. He appeared to wield the standard set of guide gear, the one given to new trainees. A sword and a knife, simple and deadly.

The one on the right, my target, had the same combo. The leader in front looked like the only experienced one. She held a pair of short axes, double bladed, with more hanging from her belt. As Selena closed, the lead guide shoved

Bryce to the ground and held her arm back to throw one of the axes.

"Duck!" I shouted. But I didn't need to. Bryce rolled and kicked the guide in the knee, knocking her off balance and forcing her to catch herself on the ground with a hand.

The guide on the right stepped up to meet Selena, his sword stabbing out in front. A maneuver that would work well against mindless spirits with no thought for their own safety. A move anyone with a functioning mind could dodge without a second thought. Selena sidestepped the strike to the right, smacking the sword aside with her cleaver and engaging with the long knife. Going for a nonlethal stab into the guides leg.

The new guide had some skill, though. He saw the strike coming in and back-stepped out of reach. Out of reach for Selena, anyway. My lash came by Selena's right side, whistled over and wrapped itself around the guide's wrist. I yanked him to the right, away from Bryce and giving Selena a clear path to my mentor.

"You don't have to fight," I said as I used the lash to throw my target to the ground. "We want Bryce. Don't want to hurt you."

"Then you shouldn't have come," said a voice to my side. The guide I'd shot put his pain behind him and stepped towards me. He swapped out his long knife for a second sword, and swung the long reach weapons at the same time. Overhead, a massive all-in attack that would be fatal if it hit.

If it hit.

I dove towards the blades, ducking into a roll to get beneath the slash. I felt the swords whistle over my coat as I came out of the somersault into a tackle, hitting the guide in the waist and bowling him over. The guide let out a pained yell as his back hit the ground and I realized he hadn't removed my crossbow bolt from his shoulder. A shoulder now planted into the hard street. I took the moment of shocked pain and used it to throw away his weapons, kicking them out of his hands to the side. They disappeared beneath the trample of spirit feet.

"Carver," Alec shouted. "A little help?"

I turned and saw Selena dragging Bryce away, helping him get up to his feet while Alec danced with the two other guides. The lead one, her twin axes moving, kept Alec on the defensive. He had to constantly shift his gauntlets to get in the way of the strikes, sparks flying every time the edges struck Alec's metal. The other guide, the sword and knife wielder, circled behind and looked for an open strike.

The guide focused too intently on Alec to see me coming. To see my lash before it wrapped around his leg and dragged it out from under him. I sent the guide crashing down, his head striking the street and falling limp.

"You're clear," I called.

Alec caught the words, blocked one more strike from the lead guide's swinging ax, and went on the offensive. Two quick jabs that forced the guide to stick her axes in front of her face for defense. A move that exposed their hafts for Alec to grab. He did so, then kicked the guide in the chest. Used his grip on the axes for added force, and as she fell back, pulled the axes free.

I turned my right, the first guide back on his feet, sword and dagger ready. Only he didn't look quite so eager to engage.

"I repeat," I spoke. "You don't have to fight this one. Back off and we'll let you go. Then you can help your friends."

The guide glanced over to his leader, who was reaching to her belt to draw new axes. She stopped as Alec moved closer, raising her own axes and showing her what might happen if she continued to fight.

"We yield," the leader said. "We're done. You can have your prisoner."

"For once, a good decision," Alec said.

"Take him now," the leader said. "But we'll send up the sparks as soon as you leave. You'll be tracked. Found. You can't hold onto him forever, and we'll make sure you share his fate."

"We could kill them, too," Selena said from the side as she used the cleaver to hack off Bryce's chains. "Hard to use a sparker when you're dead."

"How about we take the sparkers with us?" I said. "A little less lethal, I think."

I barely finished the sentence before the the guide with the bolt in his back, sitting up from the ground, stuck his hand in the air and launched the sparks. The rapid cadence, achieved by holding down the trigger and letting more more of the gas ignite, signified an emergency. Alerted any guide nearby to come for help. We were out of time.

"Run!" I yelled.

And we did.

Chapter 44

Would-be Rescuers

The four of us sprinted back through the Shambles, heading north towards the clock tower. We had to get Bryce back to where he had crossed into Riven in order for him to cross back out of it. So he could hide. I handed him my knife, giving him something to defend himself with. Kept my lash ready.

"Alec, take the lead," I said and my friend nodded. I dropped to the rear while Selena stayed near Bryce.

We ran through the streets, dodging around spirits and racing against popping sparks as guides seeing our flight launched them through the sky. Now I knew what it was like to be an angry spirit, hunted and chased throughout the gray ruins of Riven and its city. Not pleasant.

Towards the edge of the Shambles, where they bled into the park leading to the Warrens, we had our first test. A pair of older guides. Each wearing thick, damaged coats and carrying large halberds, spears with an axe edge on one side and points on top and behind. The guides looked almost identical. I knew them. A pair of twins from South America, known for working in tandem so tightly that they effectively fought as one.

"Selena, you keep Bryce moving ahead. We'll rejoin you later," Alec said. Selena listened, peeling off with Bryce to the left and into the park while Alec and I went straight for the pair.

"Alec," the first one said. "I cannot say we expected this. How many hunts have we been on together, and now you would fight against us?"

"Mateo, I did not plan this," Alec said. "It is Piotr's doing. His hands molding this conflict."

I came up beside Alec and we stood five feet away from the pair. Almost within reach of their halberds. At Alec's words, they tilted their heads, squinted their eyes.

"Piotr," Mateo said. "Piotr didn't free the prisoners. Piotr didn't hurt the other guides. Piotr didn't break Bryce free."

"Those are all symptoms," I said. "Piotr is the cause."

"Or perhaps you are," Mateo replied. "If you wish to discuss it, however, put down your weapons and come with us. We won't hurt you."

I was shaking my head before he finished. "I'm sorry Mateo, Anton. We can't."

They nodded in unison. Then set their halberds forward. I would not relish this fight.

Alec struck first, darting in as Mateo, on the left, attempted to step forward with his halberd. I cracked the lash to the right, striking towards Anton's face. The man shifted, sliding his head to the right and dodging the lash's strike. Moved towards me and brought the halberd in for a wide slash. I back-stepped, but not far enough. The point of the halberd gashed into my side and sliced along my coat. Left a searing cut in my abdomen. I winced and tried to push down the pain. No time for that here.

Anton kept coming forward, reversing his cut to swing back from the other side. If I'd had my knife, I could've tried to catch the spear. Instead, I did the only thing I could and flicked the lash again. This time, mid-swing, Anton wasn't able to dodge my strike. As his halberd's blade fell toward my side, my lash struck into his chest. The pointed ends piercing through his coat and causing Anton to stagger back, remove some of the momentum behind his cut, so that instead of being bisected, I had another long gash along my left side. Happy to make that trade.

I didn't relent, couldn't relent. As Anton stumbled back, I cracked the lash again and again. Each strike opening new holes on the guide's chest, arms, and legs. None of them truly serious, all of them debilitating. Taking away his momentum and his focus. And then Anton dropped the halberd. Let the weapon clatter to the ground at his feet. I didn't stop. Kept driving him back until I stood above his weapon, and only then did I let the lash go quiet and hang down by my side.

"I'm sorry," I said to Anton, who knelt on the ground and bled from a dozen cuts. "I'm sorry, but you didn't leave me any choice."

I turned left to see Alec take a blow from the halberd's shaft to his chin. Mateo had drawn my friend in close, and, rather than take the long swing, jerked the butt of the halberd into Alec's face. Now, as Mateo pressed the advantage, I knelt, grabbed Anton's halberd off the ground, and threw it at his brother.

It wasn't a great toss—I was no expert at throwing spears—but it was close enough. The weapon slid between Mateo's legs, biting into his thighs and knees and sending the man sprawling. Alec took advantage. Ran up and disarmed Mateo, kicking the halberd away and pinning the guide to the ground.

"Surrender," Alec said.

Mateo glared up at him, whatever spirit of fellowship that had existed between us extinguished in traitorous fashion. "You can have your victory, and we will have our revenge."

Mateo's words stuck with me as we ran through the park, catching up with Selena and Bryce on the other side. We entered the Warrens and the maze of large apartments. They would have their revenge. How many guides were saying that about us right now? Were planning to advance their own status, or avenge their friends, by taking us apart? I was starting to think there would be no way back from this. No recovery.

My days as a guide were done.

The clock tower swung into view, after another hour of dashing and hiding, ducking between stores and counters, weaving between masses of spirits on the move. Even using breaches to our advantage, drawing guides into the eruptions of angry spirits. I had no idea if some of our friends fell trying to find us. If, led into the breaches, they were overwhelmed and torn to pieces. There would be time for that later. Time to bring Piotr a reckoning for all the terrors that he had wrought.

We crossed the courtyard, around the fountain bursting Riven's water into the air, and led Bryce into the clock tower. Selena shut the doors behind us and barred them with Bryce's voulge, still in the weapon rack where he had left it.

"I can never thank you enough," Bryce said to Alec and I. "For all you've sacrificed for me, for my family. If you ever need anything . . . "

"Let's start with getting you back home," I said. "Go, cross over so we can get out of here."

Not that we knew what Bryce would find on the other side. Perhaps a jail cell. Maybe another guide or two waiting to exact some punishment. But we had to start somewhere. Give him some chance.

Bryce lay down in the bed and concentrated. I saw his eyes close and waited for his body to fade. But he didn't. Bryce sat there, in full form. After several minutes passed and Bryce still hadn't left us, I moved over. Took a close look. He breathed evenly, he hadn't sustained wounds. There shouldn't be any difficulty. Then his eyes popped open.

"They're blocking my way back," Bryce said.

"What?" I said.

"My body. They're keeping it asleep. With drugs. I felt it as I crossed back, I felt myself slipping away into a dream. If I let that happen, that I might never get back here. I might never wake up."

"Alec," I said, turning to my friend. "If he can't cross, then we have to save him on the other side. Break him free. You're the only one that can do it."

"I don't think they'll let me into the hospital, not after this," Alec said.

"Hey," Selena said from over the by the doors. "There are noises outside. I'm hearing guides talk. I think they're planning something."

I went over to the door while Alec and Bryce tried to talk strategy. Tried to look between the doors outside, but all I could see was shifting gray and a bit of the fountain. A burst of orange. A smell of smoke. I looked around us at the wood and stone chamber and realized the guides didn't have any interest in fighting us. They were going to burn us down.

Chapter 45
Smoked Out

Is there another way out?" Selena asked.

I shook my head. "Not that I know of."

I told Bryce and Alec about the burning, though the smoke coming in from under the door made it unnecessary. The gray and white smoke floated way up to the top, trapped beneath the roof. The sheer height of the building would give us some time, but it was going to get hot in here very soon.

"I can't cross back," Bryce said. "There's no way out."

"Selena and I can't either." I glanced at Alec. "Alec, go. You're the only one that can leave. Go back."

"Leave the rest of you? I'm not a coward," Alec said.

"You're no good dead," I said. I looked back towards the door, the first flicker of orange popping through near the hinges. The smoke thickened—I couldn't see the roof above anymore. "Go back. Find Bryce. Get him free."

That was a compromise Alec could accept. He slid onto the bed, closed his eyes, and faded a minute later. That left the three of us in the middle of a building rapidly turning black as flames crawled their way inside.

"Any ideas, Carver?" Selena asked.

"I've got one, but you might not like it."

"I don't think liking it matters anymore," Bryce said. "What's important is whether we make it out alive."

"That's not a guarantee," I pulled the crossbow from my back. Moved an orange bolt to the front and cranked it into firing position. "This thing is going to cause a lot of destruction. I'd stand back."

"You're going to bring down the building on top of us?" Selena asked.

"Just be ready to move," I said. "Bryce, if you want your weapon, now's the time."

Bryce nodded, went over the door and grabbed his voulge out from the locks. And winced. "It's really hot."

He ran by me as I lifted the crossbow, aimed my shot at the front wall. The door facing the fountain. If things went right, the bolt would explode and burn through, collapsing the structure and causing enough chaos for us to get away. If things went wrong, the clock tower would fall and bury us in rubble. Or we'd run right out into certain death at the hands of the guides.

I pulled the trigger.

The bolt launched out and embedded itself in the door, or what was left of it as the fire made a meal out of the building. The bolt popped and expanded in a blooming orange nova, a spreading swirl of superheated light that devoured the rest of the door. Branches launched out like electricity, tendrils snapping and grabbing on to other parts of the tower, climbing and expanding and consuming the entire front of the building in a wave of heat and light.

Around us the structure groaned. Wood and rock began to fall as supports vanished, either annihilated by the fire, the bolt, or crumbling beneath the pressure. I pulled Selena to the ground, crawled beneath the table that had for so often served little purpose inside a place we didn't spend much time. Bryce joined us, squeezing in as rocks and boards chipped off the table's surface. Heat blasted our faces as the shouts of guides wondering what was going on came through amid the crackling roars.

I took a moment to start winding the crossbow again, loading a second orange bolt. My last one. I didn't want to use it, but if we needed a way out, or a deadly distraction, then the crossbow was our only, our best chance.

Behind us, the rear structure snapped as the roof, losing its front support, listed down towards the fountain. The clock, the heaviest part of the building, pulled the roof down with it. I glanced behind, over Selena's shoulder to see the burning boards at the back of the building simply split in two. Then the roof came crashing down on top of us.

"Go to the right, now," I said. "Bring the table."

As the building collapsed we shuffled, keeping the table over our heads to catch the embers and rocks and stone as they fell. Charged towards the right wall as it folded in at us. Holes opened, ashen and orange and burning. The raging heat licking our feet and our hair and running down our throat to scorch our lungs.

"We're not going to break out," Selena said.

"Stand up and run," Bryce said. "Lead with the table."

We hit the wall in ten steps, the side of the building bulging and bending and breaking. The table smashed into it first as Bryce, Selena and I were pelted with burning chunks of wood and rock. I felt the stings of embers burning through my coat, singeing my neck, and burrowing their way into my wrist and hands. But I held on. We held on. The clock tower's wall did not.

We burst through into the open alley between the clock tower and the next building, a shower of sparks heralding our exit. A shower infinitely dwarfed by the raging inferno behind us. We dropped the table and ran, sprinting down the alley to the right. Behind the clock tower and into Riven's endless maze. Kept the blaze between us and the guides for as long as we could.

Nobody said anything for a long time. We just ran. I took the lead and gradually shifted us towards the apartment. After another hour skulking through back alleys and broken buildings, we made it. Opened the door to find Nicholas standing and staring at us. At our wrecked clothes, our burned bodies, and battered souls.

"So, did you manage to find me some iron?"

Chapter 46
To The East

I wasn't used to seeing Bryce so defeated. He collapsed on one of the few chairs Nicholas had in his lab at the bottom of the apartment building. Bryce's eyes scrolled over the surroundings without seeming to notice any of them. Nicholas, usually ready to stream an opinion, fell silent when I told him what happened.

"We still need to get you back," I said to Bryce. "Even without the clock tower, you still need to go to the spot to cross."

"I know," Bryce said. "I know. But if I'm still asleep on the other side . . . "

"Alec will see to it."

Bryce nodded, but it was the sort of nod given to stop a conversation rather than to agree. So I backed off and let Bryce confront his own demons.

"What are you going to do now?" Selena asked.

"I have to cross. It's got to be almost morning. Anna and I, we have to get to New York. Have to stop Piotr."

"And us? Do we sit here and wait for you to come back?"

I shook my head. "No, when Bryce is ready, you should try to get into the clock tower. Or what's left of it. If Alec gets him free, you may not have much time from him to cross out."

Selena and I went back up to her apartment, said our goodbyes, and then I laid down in the bed and crossed over to the other side.

Dawn broke over the town. Gold rising in a beautiful morning as woodland birds whistled. A few souls moving outside the window, beginning their daily tasks. Anna breathed slow beside me, lost in some dream. Not for much longer. I gave her what time I could as I readied. Went down to the front desk and acquired a schedule for the trains.

Twelve hours ride from here to New York. The sooner we started, the better.

"I thought you'd have had enough of trains," Anna said as we made our way to the station an hour later, *The Pine's Rest* going without payment for our night courtesy of a back door. "Weren't you a hostage the last two times you rode one?"

"Almost. With my luck, airships aren't much better. At least it's easier to get off of a train," I said. "I don't have the money to buy a car, and we don't have the time."

"Twelve hours. I've never been on a train that long."

"If we're lucky," I said. "We won't meet anyone we know. The hours will pass by in peace. I'll even get a drink."

"Maybe."

The train we were catching dwarfed the small station. A long passenger rail that stretched for car after car. I spent the last couple of dollars I had to get us tickets at the reduced rate for guides. Once we got to the city, we'd be relying on whatever we could scrounge. Whatever charity people would offer us, so long as they didn't know who we actually were.

The cars were ramshackle, and we only had a bench to ourselves. No money for a luxury compartment or any kind of sleeper cabin. Compared to the opulent airship, this was more my usual.

"Why do you think your mother gave up?" Anna asked after I told her what I'd read in my mother's diaries. "She just stayed there, in the hospital . . . "

"I don't think she had a choice," I said. "The way she wrote it, it seemed like they were coming after Katherine even before I was born. Piotr knew what I would be."

"But he couldn't use you until you grew old enough to make it over to Riven," Anna said.

"I think Piotr ran multiple schemes. I was one of his bets, and I think only at the end did he decide to use me. Or try to. He had plenty of time to let me grow."

"I want to know why," Anna said. "Why would he bother? Why risk so many guides, why risk everything to try to connect Riven to our world?"

The coffee cart came by as the train rumbled through the sloping scenery of Western Pennsylvania, rolling green hills and fields cultivated for summer crops. I grabbed a couple of mugs and took a sip. Even that little bit of normalcy helped.

"For the same reason so many others have tried the same," I said. "I think he's frightened. He's older. He doesn't want to give himself up to what comes next. I can't be sure, though. It's just a guess."

"And the other leaders? The ones he had in the Mountain?" Anna said. "They must be working together."

"Think about it," I said. "In Riven, you don't age. You don't die. You can't really get hurt for long. At least not as a spirit. Bring that back here? You could live forever."

"You don't know what would happen if the spirits came over."

"It's a risk he's willing to take."

"What would you do, in his place?" Anna asked. "Would you tear everything apart trying to find a way back?"

An easy question to say no to. A hard question if I actually thought about it. Who wouldn't want a chance to live forever, to see and do everything without a care for your physical health? On the other hand, the reason we were trying to stop Piotr was that opening the gateway could destroy everything we ever loved. Could make both Riven and our world fall apart.

"I think I would want what Piotr wants," I said. "But I hope I'd have the strength to resist. Would you?"

Now it was Anna's turn to look out the window and take a moment to think. Were we the same as Piotr, only without the power and position?

"I'm a selfish person," Anna said. "I do a lot of things for me, and to help accomplish my goals. I don't think I could do this. I don't think I could justify it to myself and say the chance of a strange, endless life would be worth this risk."

I nodded. "Only eleven more hours to go."

I wouldn't mind the wait.

Chapter 47

Big Apple, Little Chance

Chicago was not a small city. It had its share of tall buildings and sparkling design. New York was something else altogether. A showcase for experimental architecture, in what the mad magicians of metal and glass could come up with. Structures of all shapes soared up and down the skyline, looping and curving at times through each other.

Elevated halls, supported by filled balloons, like stationary zeppelins, held sway between buildings and allowed people to cross without descending the many stories to the ground below. Lights and sounds splashed in the train windows and echoed through our compartment.

An endless plethora of motorized vehicles, blowing horns, and hidden growls and rumbles that make up the background symphony of any bustling place.

Anna and I made our way out of Penn Station and slipped on our masks, the first time since leaving Chicago that I bothered to put it on. Pollution, it seemed, tied a common thread between our cities.

"Where do you think they're holding the conference?" I asked Anna as she stared at the chaos around us.

"I'd say we follow the motorcades," Anna said, pointing.

I tracked her eyes and saw the scattered cars emblazoned with various flags. The squat vehicles carted ambassadors and presidents through the traffic and throngs of people towards their destination. Even though we were walking, we easily kept pace.

In Chicago, downtown taxis kept the streets clear. If you walked over one of the lines, you were liable to get hit. In New York, there were simply too many people. No automated taxis, only the human variety. An endless array of cars and horses, walkers and riders.

As we neared what looked to be a large square, I heard the cries of a nearby newspaperman. Shouting out the evening edition, including tonight's various speeches and the schedule for tomorrow. I pulled us towards the crier and, after begging Anna to pay for a copy, grabbed the newsprint.

"He's not here tonight," I said looking at the lists of politicians from around the world. "Tomorrow, though, Piotr has the evening to himself."

"What are you thinking?"

"Look around," I said. "There's so many people, so many police. There's no way we're going to be able to take him out on the street. But if we can tail him, maybe we can find out where he's staying."

"You're starting to talk like a sneak," Anna said.

"Maybe you're rubbing off on me," I replied.

"I can only hope so," Anna said. "If we're not going after Piotr tonight, we need somewhere to stay. And I'm broke."

"That makes two of us."

We stood in the street, Anna reading through the paper and me scanning the crowd. Trying to think of something to do. I couldn't lean on my guide contacts; the New York group would turn me in the moment I showed my face. We could just wander the streets until the next day, but I didn't relish the idea of taking on Piotr after going all night without rest.

"How about this?" Anna lifted the paper and pointed to a printed ad calling out services for connecting people with their lost relatives. Either here or in Riven.

"Sneaks?"

"You might be wanted by the guides," Anna said. "But I'm still a sneak, and on their good side. I think."

"Do you even know them?"

"Do you know every guide?" Anna replied. "Come on, let's go."

The ad noted an office in the lower east side of Manhattan. A solid twenty block walk from where we were now, but I relished the exercise. Taking in the sights and sounds of a different sort of metropolis. The buildings here were taller, more compressed in the smaller landscape. The sounds were different too: mixed accents and calls for foods of different types. There was a feel of motion here that I didn't have back home.

There were similarities: Mechs stood everywhere. The conference boosted security, made patrols even more prolific than in Chicago. Masks were the status symbol of the day here too, with the wealthier groups sporting artistic arrangements over their faces and the less well-off going with colored cloth filters.

The reaction to seeing a pair of guides was the same sort of nervous caution. Crowds parted around Anna and I as we walked along. Eyes crawled up and down my coat.

Eventually, with the sun vanishing beneath the horizon and the city basking us in bright lights, we made it to a squat building that seemed, quivering beneath the towering construction around it, not long for this world. The office and the apartments above belonged to the sneaks, or, as the sign outside declared, *New York's Finest Finders*. The door was unlocked, the inside lit by a plethora of lights.

"Look, they have electricity," I said to Anna.

"They have money," Anna said. "Laurence and I do what we can with what we have."

Inside, we were greeted by a row of chairs in a room ringed with doors. Private hideaways where clients could talk with a sneak without worrying about being overheard.

"Can I help you both?" said the woman as she came out of the back hallway. Unlike Anna, who made her way in a casual outfit, the sneak wore a professional dress. Ready for business, and for a certain type of clientele that I didn't think would bother leveraging a sneak.

"I have a favor to ask," Anna said. At the woman's nod we launched into our story. Filtered out details like bringing down the airship. Whittled it down to the two of us needing to spend the night in the city and not having the funds to do so.

When Anna finished the woman told us to wait a minute, and disappeared back through the door.

"Do you think she bought it?" I said.

"Not at all," Anna said. "But she'll come back with an offer."

"With an offer?"

"Sneaks don't give things away for free," Anna said. "My guess is if we can't pay, they'll find something else for us to do. Maybe you can use your mask and scare away bad clients."

"Very funny."

The woman returned and waved us back with her. We followed; through a bland hallway and back into the start of the apartments. A broad room with a small kitchen, table and chairs. A radio playing the current speaker from the conference. On the table sat three other sneaks, all in suits and collared shirts.

"You are a guide, aren't you?" the woman said after bidding us to sit down. I nodded in reply. "Then you know Riven is getting more dangerous lately. We've even lost one of us."

"I'm sorry," I said. "That's why we're here. We're trying to end this war."

"What I don't understand," the woman said, "is why you're coming to us when you should have plenty of guides you can turn to for a night in the city."

"We're trying to keep it quiet," Anna said.

"Why don't you tell us why you're really here," one of the other sneaks, a thin older man said. "Or we'll send you out that door right now."

I looked over the group, saw only curiosity, not hostility. A willingness to believe.

"We need to stop the leader of the guides from breaking Riven apart."

Chapter 48
A Fee

"Of the ridiculous things I've heard today," the thin man said. "This one tops them all. Trying to kill the leader of the guides? Why?"

"Because he wants Riven to splinter and send the spirits back here," I said.

"Ludicrous," said another of the sneaks. "That would be suicide."

"Not if you're already dead," I said. "Then, you could wander the world as a spirit. Live forever. Or so the thinking goes."

"I've never heard of that happening before," the thin man said. "Where's the proof that it would even work?"

I shook my head. There wasn't any proof. Not that I knew of.

"Why take the chance?" Anna spoke up. "If Piotr succeeds, then our world will be overrun. If it doesn't work, if he can't make a gate, then Riven will still be too dangerous for anyone to cross to. You'll be out of a job."

"Now there's an angle I can understand," the woman we'd met at the front said. "Regardless, all you're asking for is an overnight. That, we can provide. For a favor."

"A favor," I said.

"We have a client with a special request," the woman said. "She can cross over into Riven, and knows where she wants to go. However, Riven is a dangerous place to be right now. Too dangerous for us. An experienced pair of guides, though?"

"So we take this client of yours to somewhere in Riven, and you'll let us stay?" Anna said, then glanced at me.

"We can do that," I said. There wasn't any way an escort job would be difficult. Not with what we'd already been through.

"Then it's agreed," the woman said. "Silas, would you mind fetching Honora and telling her we can proceed this evening?"

Silas, the thin man, nodded, stood up and left the room. The woman turned back to us.

"If you wouldn't mind, I can show you to your rooms. I imagine you'll need to get your gear on the other side. So if you want to get started?"

"Launching right into it?" I said.

"I don't know where you came from, guide, but in this city we do not waste time," the woman replied.

"Fine with me."

They set Anna and I up in a pair of individual rooms, twin beds set in blank-walled rectangles. At least the pillows were soft, the blankets good. The sneaks might not have cared about the ambient decoration, but they put quality where it mattered.

As I prepped to cross over, I realized that we hadn't ever asked for their names, and they had never asked for ours. I suppose if you're going to work with criminals, it might be better to remain anonymous.

I showed up in Riven next to Anna, an alleyway somewhere close to the ruin of the clock tower. I recognized the buildings, ones I'd wandered past countless times in my hunts through the gray world.

"To the apartment?" I said, and Anna agreed.

Both of us noted where we'd come in, as we'd have to head back to this spot to return to New York. On the ground around us, trash had been scattered. Broken beds and shredded sheets. A pair of dirty mattresses leaning against the wall. Guides took the time to set up true bases. Built and maintained spaces meant for frequent crossings. This, this was meant to look random and dirty enough to pass for an accident. I only picked up the garbage's true purpose because I'd crossed over to this spot.

Anna and I made our way through the alleys and avenues to the apartment. Other guides and the occasional spirit wandered by, causing us to duck out of sight. Still, compared with the chaos of Bryce's escape, I enjoyed the walk. The quiet, empty streets a welcome reprieve from the crowds of New York.

"Are you still doing all right?" Anna asked as we continued. "About your parents?"

"I'm hanging in there," I said. "It would be worse, except I spent most of my life alone. Now it's just back to the usual."

"I suppose," Anna said, though her tone implied otherwise.

"You? I haven't noticed tears, and you've kept composed."

"Now if that isn't the nicest thing anyone's ever said to me . . . " Anna laughed. "I keep it to myself. Nurture their memory."

"Sorry," I said. "Sometimes I talk like a hammer."

"Sometimes?"

Anna kept her grief to herself. Bottled it up and hid it. I wasn't all that different. Every day brought one moment after another that I wanted to share with Graham and Katherine. In Riven or otherwise. Saving Bryce, getting out of the burning clock tower, I could imagine talking every detail over with my parents and earning their praise, enduring their loving criticism.

At the same time, it had been easy to fall back into the habit of relying on me and me alone. Taking in the situation and depending on my own sense to get me out of it. I didn't *need* Graham and Katherine for me to survive, but I wanted them sharing my world.

When the two of us walked into the apartment, Bryce, Selena, and Nicholas were bent over the scientist's workbench. Piecing together some new weapon or other invention.

"We're back!" I announced, and the group turned around. "And we need our stuff."

Chapter 49
First Crossings

If there was a moment when I felt that Bryce was no longer my mentor, it came when he let me go with Selena and Anna. Let me leave the apartment armed and ready for adventure, but without him. Bryce said he had to wait for Alec, as the guide was still working to see whether he could locate Bryce on the other side and free him. If Alec could cause a large enough distraction for Bryce to cross over.

On my own. The leader of our little band.

We headed back towards the trash-littered spot in the alley near the clock tower. Where the child would appear at some point soon. Selena, her cleaver idly hanging from her left hand, whistled an old song as we walked. Anna, for her part, seemed lost in deep thoughts.

I didn't say anything. Plenty of my own thinking to do. I could feel the conflict with Piotr barreling to a close. A fight that would likely leave only one of us left. The questions niggling at my head concerned what would happen after? Would the guides rebel or scatter, letting angry spirits run amok? Would they rally behind me or someone else? Stand up to the dead and force Riven back to sanity or collapse?

Of course, Piotr might cut me in half and solve all my problems, but that wasn't a fun path to go down.

"This is the spot, right?" Anna said, and I blinked, realized she was right. Same alleyway, same dirty mattresses.

"So we wait?" Selena said, then glanced at Anna. "Is this what you did before? Took people on trips through Riven?"

"Sometimes." Anna had a defensive edge to her voice. "Only if they could cross over, though. Most of the time it was find and report back."

"Running errands, you mean?"

I laughed. "Selena might've picked up some of my old prejudices."

"I noticed," Anna said. "They were only errands if the client wanted them to be. When you're helping someone heal an emotional wound, or get a last conversation with a loved one, that's not so trivial."

There was a rustling noise, a scattered clinking as bits and pieces of rock and junk fell off their pile next to us. Climbing from beneath a sheet; a dark girl of no more than twelve looked out.

"They said to hide, so I hid," the girl said. "They said there'd be a man and a woman, were they talking about you?"

"Are you Honora?" I asked and the girl nodded. "Then we're the ones you're looking for."

"Where are your parents?" Anna said, and Honora pointed, down the alley and away to the north.

"Why don't you hop in line behind Anna here, and you just tell me which way to go as we walk?" I said, leading us off. No reason to waste time. The sooner the girl could cross back, the less chance of something terrible happening to her.

North of the clock tower, the city broke into a crumbling range of parks and clusters of homes. A place that could have been, would have been a ritzy residential area if the ponds weren't dusty and dry, the homes razed, and the trees shattered bits of their former selves. Of the parts of Riven that had suffered over the centuries, the north had fallen the farthest.

"When did you first cross over?" Anna continued her conversation with Honora, peppering the girl with question after question. At first I didn't understand why, but then I noticed Honora was paying more attention to her answers than to the ruins around us. Ignoring the occasional spirit wandering by. The sparks bursting in the air above as guides called to each other.

"Three years ago," Honora said. "It was scary. I didn't understand."

"I bet," I muttered. Remembered my own first time vividly. I'd been seven, curled up on the couch, the only place to sleep in the apartment where my current foster parent lived. A grouchy old guide, Morton, who, his age and general annoyance with everything notwithstanding, kept a focused eye on me at all times.

Looking back, I realized that the old man kept me on that couch for a reason. It was tied to the top of an apartment in the Warrens, a room with one door that he'd locked from the outside. When I launched myself into Riven, without a clue of what I was doing, I'd been safe. The windows were barred; metal rods jammed into the walls. I could only stare out at the city below me, until he opened the door.

"Did you talk to your parents about it?" Anna asked.

"They told me it was just a bad dream," Honora said. "That I didn't have to worry."

Morton hadn't played games with me. That same night, when he'd opened the door, he'd given me a knife almost half as tall as I was. Told me that, no matter how old I was, every night had a chance of killing me. Morton, in his black, long coat and crag-covered face, had glared at me until I held the knife like I meant to wield it. The first of many lessons.

"Mine did too," Anna said. "Only you knew that wasn't true, right?"

Honora held out her left arm and nodded to a vicious twisting scar. "I learned."

My first encounter with an angry spirit happened more than a year later. A year of crossing into that locked room and waiting for Morton to let me out. We'd avoided any real guide work in that time. Exploring, taking twisting routes that I'd thought were planned but, really, was Morton's work with a resonator to avoid any danger.

That night, not long after I'd turned eight years old, we stopped outside of a busted up store. Bare shelves broken and leaning on each other, ash flakes clustering in the corners. Morton had turned to me, taken one of his constant rattling sighs, as though dealing with me was a burden ill-promised and unearned.

"In there," Morton said. "Is a trial. Your first real test. Do you think you're ready?"

"Yes," I said with a child's invincibility backing my voice.

"You're not," Morton replied. "You're going to get chewed up. Torn to pieces. If you're lucky, I'll be fast enough to save you. If you're not . . . "

Morton had probably meant that line to leave me scared and cautious. Afraid of the consequences. Except after a year of enduring Morton's endless dire premonitions and grumping growls, I wanted to prove to him that I wasn't useless.

"So then what did you do?" Anna asked Honora.

"I learned to hide," Honora said. "Did you?"

"All the time," Anna replied. "I still do."

I had ventured into the store slowly, holding the knife out in front of me; a shield as much as a weapon. From the back of the place, hidden behind a counter, I heard a voice muttering to itself. Quiet whispers that blurted, every so often, a single syllable. I placed every step carefully, measuring the distance and letting the soles of my boots land evenly on the floor.

The counter itself was the best part of the store. Still more or less intact, still with a glass case. Nothing but empty shelves inside, but I could see through. Could catch a glimpse of the creature beyond.

My first angry spirit sat on the floor, a boy not much older than I was. His legs splayed out and, in his hands, he held onto what looked like some broken pieces of wood. He moved them together, pressing them at angles into each other. Trying to build something.

I could finally make out his words. A series of names, repeated to himself over and over. Back then I didn't understand. Now, I've heard spirits do the same thing. A way of remembering parts of their lives as Riven began to take it away.

"When did your parents pass?" Selena asked Honora.

"Only a week ago," Honora said. "They made me promise to come see them."

"So that's why you're here?"

Honora nodded. "They were real sick. They couldn't get out of bed, and so they said they would say goodbye here. Where they could stand."

The boy's eyes had blazed with the pale fire. I remembered staring at that face for an entire minute, taking in the flickering anger. The contorting mouth. Then I glanced back towards the shop's entrance, saw Morton standing there, saw his grim nod.

I went around the counter, held the knife steady, and went up to the boy. He didn't even notice I was there until I was nearly on top of him, the knife an inch away from his chest. Then his face met mine, and he fell silent.

We stared at each other for a long beat. And then he lunged for me, his hands grasping for my face. I yelled, fell back, and stuck the knife forward out of desperation. Felt it bite into something.

"Twist the hilt, Reed!" Morton had called from the other side of the counter.

I felt the boy's fingers brush my face as I turned my wrist. Opened my eyes in time to see the blue fire spread from the knife, cover the angry spirit. Saw the boy's snarling face fall into slack-jawed nothing.

"How do you know where to find them?" Anna said. "Riven's a big place?"

"I told them where I hid," Honora said. "My favorite spot when I crossed over."

"How much further is it?" Selena asked.

"Right there," Honora pointed to a large grove of dead trees, and within them, a small shed. Its wooden sides were sagging and the roof had a small hole, but otherwise the place seemed intact.

Morton had dragged me up, forced me out to the street to watch the boy walk away into the distance.

"He's going to the Cycle now," Morton said. "Where he's supposed to be. You did well,

Reed. Seems you might be ready for the next step."

A week later, I'd left Morton's couch for good and boarded a bus to Chicago, where I met a man named Bryce.

Chapter 50

Say Goodbye

I opened the crooked door to the shed. Inside, amid filtered rays of gray light and scattered bits of rubble, stood a pair of spirits looking at me with calm, understanding eyes. No sign of pale fire, no need to keep my hand on my lash.

"Are you Honora's parents?" I asked.

"We are," replied the woman. "Is she with you?"

That statement alone; a cognizant reply to a question, did as much as anything to calm my fears. Spirits that were on the verge of losing themselves didn't have that much composure. Didn't care what questions were being asked.

"She is," I said, then waved Honora in. "They're all yours."

Anna stayed in the shed with the girl while Selena and I took up a casual post outside.

"I'm happy for her," Selena said.

"Rare," I replied. "The two of them happened to cross close enough to each other to keep themselves sane over here. That's lucky."

"I doubt Honora would see it that way."

I nodded. Doubted that she would. Tough to wager a few extra days with a dying parent against the chance to say goodbye to both of them in Riven. I knew which option I'd take, though.

"Do you think your children ever tried to see you?" I asked Selena.

"I don't know if they can cross over," Selena said. "If they could, if they can, then I hope they moved on. I'm not the mother they knew anymore."

I let the thread drop and Selena didn't try to pick it up. Her children were a sensitive topic.

Selena never mentioned them. I didn't know their names, what they looked like. For her, maybe, it was a piece of a life she didn't have anymore. We moved on to the Cycle, what Anna and I were planning for Piotr.

The shed door swung open behind me. Anna led Honora by us, the girl wiping away tears but otherwise standing tall.

"Her parents have something to ask you," Anna said to me. "We'll take Honora back and you can catch up with us."

I raised an eyebrow, but Anna dodged it and looked down at Honora, gave her a gentle push to start the walk back.

"Want me to stay?" Selena asked and I shook my head.

"I don't think this will take long," I replied.

Back inside the shed, I shut the door behind me. Honora's parents stared at me, their faces calm and set. Again her mother spoke first, after she had grabbed her husbands hands and held them tight.

"We would ask that you let us go," she said. "We have said our goodbyes, and have no wish to spend another moment in this wretched place."

The father nodded in agreement.

"You're certain?" I asked. "Together, you two might be able to hold on for some time. Perhaps see Honora again?"

"We can hear it," the father said. "Feel it pressing against us. If we are to go, then I would have it be by our own choice. I do not want to turn into an animal."

Now the mother nodded.

I used the knife. Twisted the hilt, a light poke into their arms, and the fire washed them away.

As I left the shed, I twisted the door. Blocked it with some of the fallen wood from the dead trees. Hopefully it would delay their walk to the Cycle long enough for Honora to cross away. The last memory of her parents would be as they wanted it.

We went back into the city, and let Honora cross over on a dirty mattress in the alley. Anna followed, giving Selena her gear. I handed Selena mine too, so that she looked like a caricature, loaded down with a ridiculous number of weapons. Except, as a spirit, she couldn't really get tired.

"When will you come back?" Selena asked.

"We're going to try and handle Piotr tomorrow night. Hopefully, after that, I'll find a way to cross in and give an update," I said. "If things go will, it will be over."

"Then the real battle begins," Selena said, her eyes flashing up to a set of exploding yellow sparks overhead.

"We'll save it," I said. "With all of the other guides? We can hold Riven together."

"Remember when I said I didn't like this place? How I wanted a way out?"

"You nearly got me killed trying to find it."

She'd led me right to Graham and his vicious hammer. To be fair, Selena had also led Alec and Bryce to my rescue, but still . . .

"Sorry about that," Selena replied. "What I'm trying to say is that now, rather than feeling trapped by Riven, I feel like I'm a part of it. I'm participating in this world. I've found a new life, Carver, and I don't want to lose it."

Chapter 51

Talking and Tracking

When I crossed back from Riven, it was mid-morning. Anna and the other sneaks were talking over breakfast, swapping strategies for dodging guides and breaches. All of them paused as I sat down, until Silas pushed over the plate of bread and cheese they were splitting. I stayed quiet as the conversation resumed. Let the words wash over me as I kept turning over ways to catch Piotr in my mind.

The day went by fast after that. Anna and I explored what we could of the city, keeping an eye out for signs of Piotr or other guides. Trying to keep our own heads down. The airship crash was all over the newspapers and blaring radios, but nobody had tried to pin it on us yet. Blamed as a mechanical failure.

You saw that all the time. Machines going awry were as common as each new day. A standard part of life. What wouldn't have been, what would have attracted more attention, was a claim that a pair of criminals had made their way into the engine room and brought down the ship. Why attract controversy when none was needed?

Eventually we made it to a wide square where, in the middle, beneath a large marble dome and surrounded by a colonnade covered in the flags of all the states, a banner welcomed the participants in the world peace conference. The sun dipped low. Piotr's assigned speaking slot would be up soon.

"I guess it's time," I said.

"My feet could use a rest anyway," Anna replied.

We walked up to the entrance, a long series of thin steps that nonetheless brought us high enough to stare over the heads of the crowds shifting back and forth behind us. A large array of security stood in front, holding batons and wearing the deep blue uniforms of New York police.

"You think they're looking for us?" Anna asked.

"I don't think so," I said. "Why would they think we'd come here?"

"Oh, I don't know, maybe because we crashed an airship heading to New York?"

"Just act confident," I said. "Nobody's blamed us for the crash yet."

The confidence act got us to the front of the line, to the point where a police officer, holding a large set of papers with names on it, stared at us and shook his head. "You're not on the list, you're not getting in."

"We're late additions," Anna tried.

"Sorry," the officer replied. "If you're with an embassy, or you have a sponsor, get them to come and add your name. Then I'll let you in. If you're just looking to listen, though, they'll play the broadcasts at any of the bars around here."

The officer gestured at a couple of establishments down the steps. Anna and I chose a place by the name of *The Guided Spirits*. It seemed fitting; a bar themed after Riven. It was empty inside, perhaps owing to the slightly early hour and the entertainment on offer. Speakers around the small bar, a place full of wood furniture and gray, speckled walls, blasted out one windy speech after another.

"How are we going to catch Piotr from here?" Anna asked.

"All we need to know is when he leaves." I waved down the bartender. "Then we can follow them to his hotel, and try to get in there."

"With your bare hands?" Anna raised an eyebrow.

"With whatever I can find. We've come this far. We can't stop now."

The bartender gave us a nod, and a free drink. For being guides, he said. I asked how he named the place and the man said that he'd flamed out of guide training as a child, but still remembered how Riven looked. How it felt. He asked if it'd changed it all in the decades since he last crossed, before they blinded him to keep him safe.

I told him no.

The speakers burst with static, a change in the presenters. Whomever was leading the evening's schedule announced that the next speaker came not from any country, but was perhaps the most impacted of all of them.

"Piotr's talking," I said. "I can't believe it."

"What do you bet that he'll talk about opening the gate and sending all the spirits back from Riven?"

"If that happens, I think the police might do our job for us."

Over the speakers, we heard the gruff tones of Piotr's voice. Thanking the various countries for attending, and that he hoped this summit could prove to be a beginning to ending the deadly war.

"All of you have seen your sons and daughters part ways with their lives in this bloody and miserable fighting," Piotr said. "Yet, for everyone that gives themselves in service to their country, my guides pay an added price. In a war that you cannot see, we are trying to keep all of you safe. Throwing ourselves into harm's way day after day, night after night to send the very souls you lose to the Cycle.

"Remember, as the negotiations continue, that every piece of land, every town, every treaty becomes worthless if Riven falls. If the angry dead return to take what they've lost."

I took a slow sip of vodka. Burning anger bubbled up as Piotr continued to rail about the threats posed by Riven's collapse. The man who wanted to bring about that fall doing everything he could to prevent it. Then again, there was a reason the guides followed him without question. Piotr was a leader. He knew when and what to say.

After another ten minutes outlining all of the dire consequences, Piotr concluded his speech with a plea for peace. Applause played him off the stage. The announcer declared the evening's events concluded.

And our night began.

Chapter 52

The Attack

I thought it would be harder to find Piotr in the masses leaving the conference center. Hordes of people in light and dark jackets, despite the warm weather. Masks on. But Piotr stood tall, and his gold and blue-tipped mask didn't fully cover the white hair streaming down from his head and over his shoulders. Anna and I stood outside the bar and watched as he made his way down towards a line of waiting motorcars. And then ignored them. Continued to walk along down the avenue, pursued by a gaggle of reporters throwing questions.

"Maybe he's got a close hotel," Anna said.

"Easier for us, then," I replied.

We started off, careful to keep some distance between us and our quarry. Not that it would've mattered. The sidewalk was so crushed with people, even at this time of the evening, the sun having set and lights popping on, that recognizing a random person seemed a ludicrous idea. If not for that flowing white mane, there would've been no tracking Piotr.

After several blocks Piotr turned and held up a hand. The reporters, along with their note-taking recorders, paused. I heard Piotr tell them no further comments, and good night. The man we were after vanished inside of his hotel.

We followed.

The *Avalon* looked as if Ezra's had transformed into a large hotel. Instead of a single crimson bar, dark wood made up most of the interior. A marble floor greeted our steps and a fleet of doormen attended to guests going in and out or seeking direction. Restaurants bordered us on either side of the lobby, places well beyond the small amount of cash the sneaks had given us for last night's work.

We drew eyes as we went in, our dirty cloaks and haggard appearance doing us no favors with a crowd looking for confirmation of their own high status. Not that I cared. I had no interest in the puffery of the city. The only thing I wanted was walking up the grand central staircase in front of us.

I'm not sure what made Piotr look our way. A sound I didn't hear. Or one of those itchy feelings of eyes on your back. Either way, the leader of the guides paused his climb and turned to us, rested his eyes on mine as we stood inside the door looking back at him.

"Is he going to run?" Anna asked.

"I don't think so." I didn't know why I thought that, just that the idea of Piotr, in his ornate official cloak, smothered with gold outlines of the guide's insignia, taking off and huffing up the stairs seemed ridiculous.

A moment later Piotr turned back and continued walking up. We followed. No reason to hide now. No hope of pretending. Piotr himself climbed slowly, giving us time to catch up and see every time he chose to take the stair to another level. Going higher and higher.

He stopped at the eighth floor, one beneath the roof. Turned and looked back at us at the landing below him.

"Carver Reed," Piotr said. "You've proved quite difficult to get rid of."

"Through no lack of trying on your part," I replied.

"I'm only doing what is best," Piotr said. "Riven is collapsing, and we need a way to remove the pressure."

"Letting spirits cross back over isn't going to help anything."

"Ah yes, because you are an expert on such things. Doubting me, someone who has all the wisdom of the guides that came before plotting his course."

"Can we shut him up already?" Anna muttered.

I took a running start, pushing myself ahead of Anna. For two reasons. One, I didn't want her as implicated in this. If possible, Anna could get away without drawing too much attention to herself. Without ruining her life the way I was destroying mine. And two, I really wanted Piotr to myself. For my parents.

Piotr turned and ran down the hall as I charged. I hit the top of the stairs and rebounded after him. Heard Anna pounding the carpet behind me.

"Why are you running?" I yelled after Piotr. "If you are so truly trying to save the world, then why hide your intentions?"

"Because they would never understand," Piotr replied. He abruptly turned to a room, jammed a key into a lock and twisted it. Open the door as I reached him. Pulled me inside as I grabbed his shoulder.

I heard the door slam behind me as we went into the room, a spacious suite with multiple beds and lanterns hanging from the ceiling. Outside the windows, Manhattan sprawled forth. I saw it for only a moment before I felt other hands pulling me off of Piotr.

I threw an elbow behind me, felt it catch a chin. The hands let go of my right arm and I swung a punch at the guy holding on to my left. He caught it, and I recognized that face. Bloodied and battered. Scarred and angry.

Derringer shoved me back against a dresser, rattling the radio sitting on top. Brought his left hand in a hook towards my face, which I ducked and countered with a waist high tackle. I heard a click, the door locking as I shoved Derringer into a chair. He toppled over on the ground, groaning. And then I felt a point sticking into my back. The sharp pain of a knife kissing my skin.

"You'll want to stop now, Carver," Piotr said, sparing a glance for Derringer. "Or Polk ends your life right here."

I froze. Tried to look around the room and see if there was an easy out. Something I could use to turn the tables. Until then, I could ask questions. Keep them distracted.

"You and Derringer are impossible to kill," I said to the man behind me. "How did you even get here?"

"That reporter told us everything," Polk said. "A knife to the throat was enough to open him up. We caught the overnight train. It seems you and Anna were too slow."

That night we spent in the hotel. That had given them an edge. Nothing we could do about it now.

"Doesn't look like your travel did Derringer any favors," I said. "Are you as messed up as he is? A horror show for the eyes?"

I felt the knife shift, Polk's muscles tense. If I could turn fast enough, could take the blade away . . . I took a breath.

"Carver, if you move," Piotr said, nodding to Derringer. "He'll shoot you. No matter how fast you think you are, you can't beat both of them."

Derringer pulled a revolver from his jacket and leveled it at me. Caught between a knife and a bullet. Not exactly how I wanted this to go.

Chapter 53

Forced Over

They sat me down on the bed. Derringer going to the bathroom to clean up while Polk kept the revolver leveled at my face. Piotr stood in front of me, hands at his side and looking almost sad at the situation.

"The strange thing is, Carver," Piotr said. "When I made you the head guide of Chicago, I meant it. I thought you were up to the task. After Graham and Barth failed, I'd all but given up at using you as a way out. Riven is collapsing, but it would still need strong guides to keep the flood in control once the spirits had broken Riven apart. I thought you could be one of them."

"Thanks for the consideration."

"Now, though," Piotr said, "even if you could help me, your death would be warranted. You caused terror, and hurt to people both in this world and others. You injured guides, civilians. Bound spirits rather than sending them to the Cycle. By any measure, Carver, you are a criminal. One that deserves nothing less than death."

"And yet, all of this is because of your actions," I said.

"Yes, yes," Piotr said. "Blame me. I'm the source of all your problems. It sounds satisfying, doesn't it? To throw all the wrongs in your life on the shoulders of someone else? Let me tell you, Carver, what feels better. Owning your failures, owning your successes. I will give you one more chance to redeem your life. Cross over, find me at the Mountain, and give me the chance to save Riven. There is still time for us to relieve the pressure. To use your miracle to help us control Riven's end."

"What if I say no?" My mind swirled through options and opportunities, ways to get out of the bed and make a break for it. I could dive through the window, plummet to the street below and splatter all over the ground. I could make a desperate grab for Polk's gun, but even if I managed to wrest it from his hand, I'd take at least one bullet. Would still be outnumbered.

I didn't know where Anna had gone, but I was glad she hadn't followed. Glad Piotr didn't seem to care about her. If this was truly the end, then I hoped that she could find a happy way to spend her last days before spirits overran the Earth .

"A simple answer," Piotr said. "First, Polk here will shoot you. Then we will track down Bryce and Alec; make them pay for aiding you. We will send Anna, that sneak which you insisted on making into a guide, to receive a cleansing. At the end, when the spirits break the Cycle and open a path out of Riven, all you will have caused is suffering."

"You've thought about this."

"It gives me no small amount of satisfaction," Piotr said. "Now please, choose."

I looked at the barrel of Polk's gun, Piotr's face, and decided the only way I had a chance to help my friends was on the other side. A useless death here would mean nothing. So I closed my eyes, focused on Riven, and crossed over.

Except I felt myself getting pulled. Pulled far away. This bed had been used before, had already been tainted and tied to a place in Riven. A place well beyond any I had ever been. And when I opened my eyes in the gray otherness, I was lost.

Chapter 54

The Fields

All around me, reaching nearly up to my chin, were long white stalks of grain. They shifted back and forth in Riven's breeze. The swooshing sound coupled with nothing else, the near silence playing into my ears as I searched the surroundings. I'd crossed over outside the city, that much was obvious.

Laurence, the sneak that worked with Anna, had once shown me the maps in their office. Their basement lair beneath the building being constructed in Chicago, a city I might never see again. He said east of Riven's city lies an endless field of grain. Stalks like these. I was likely in that field, somewhere.

I couldn't see a skyline, no crumbling towers on the horizon. No landmark beyond the shifting stalks. Beneath me, the hard ground felt the same as in the forest. Dirt overlaid with dead grass. I had no weapons, nothing other than the shirt and trousers that crossed over every time. The coat I brought with me.

Still, I was in Riven. That gave me options. I fell within myself and reached out. Focused on the bond between myself and Selena. Sent my emotions soaring across our great divide and connected with her. Felt her warm rush of happiness that I held and treasured.

"Where are you?" Selena said through our bond. "Did you find Piotr?"

I told her the story. By turns experienced her shock, and her anger. I'm sure she felt mine as well.

"So now I'm here," I said. "Wherever here is."

"You're supposed to meet them at the Mountain?" Selena said.

"That's what Piotr told me," I replied. "I don't think he expected me to cross here."

"Then use it, Carver. Use the time to think of something. To find a way to win."

"I'll try, but I'm curious," I said. "Someone crossed in this bed, someone brought it here. Why?"

Selena didn't have an answer. I couldn't get a direction, so after a minute I decided to walk. To brush aside the grains with my hands and wander through the endless field. The stalks felt dry but not brittle. Hard and strong. For being dead, or whatever they were in this world, the grain wasn't ready to fold.

"How are the two of you hanging on?" I asked Selena as I walked.

"It's getting harder and harder to leave," Selena said. "More breaches are forming every day. The guides are everywhere. If I have to leave, I can wear my coat and take my cleaver, and they don't notice that I'm not one of them."

"Do you think Riven is falling apart?"

"As we know it? Yes."

"Then am I doing the wrong thing? Should I give it up? Find Piotr and let him use me to open his gate?"

Selena stayed quiet after that one. Let me wander further underneath that unchanging cloud-covered sky. If I hadn't felt the stream of conflicting emotions coming through our bond then I might've thought she hadn't heard the question.

"He wants to bring himself back," Selena said. "He said as much to you. That's not what's meant for us, when we go to Riven. You took an oath to be a guide, one whose mission is to see spirits safely to their end. If you are who you say you are, then it is your job to make sure Piotr doesn't open the gate."

"Strikes me as almost petty," I said. "If he could save Riven at the cost of my life, why shouldn't I give it to him?"

"You don't know that," Selena said. "And he's already sacrificed how many guide lives? How much time and energy? If he had spent all of this time wrangling more spirits, putting together a strategy to stop the war in your world, then perhaps this wouldn't be a problem."

I nodded, even though she couldn't see it. Piotr's gate might save Riven in the short-term, but at what terrible cost to the rest of the world?

A line blurred in the distance, a part of the horizon that didn't match the rest. Darker than gray, and flowing upward. Smoke from a fire. A target.

"I found something," I said. "Thanks for the talk."

"That's all you can say to me?" Selena said.

"I'm sorry. Thanks, as ever, for being there. For making me understand that I'm not always as evil as I seem to be."

"You never are. Go, find your way back to me."

Chapter 55

An Ancient Soul

A small hut sat beneath the trail of smoke, made from stalks of the dead wheat. In front burned the fire, a large stacking of grain going up as the flames made their way through them. More slowly than I would've expected, but this was Riven. Natural laws didn't always apply.

The owner of the fire, or least I assumed that's what she was, stood off to the side and watched the stalks burn. She wore a fine coat, the same full-body length as the one I sported. Only it looked older, poorer craftsmanship of a simpler time. Rough cloth woven together with less of the precision than modern machines produced for us. Its hood hid her face, and the only way I knew it was a she at all was the hair coming out from the hood's bottom, long and silver, and her hands reaching out of the sleeves and clasping in front of her.

"It's been a long time since I've had a visitor here," the woman said without looking up from the fire.

"Where is here?" I asked.

"Names should be exchanged before questions are asked," the woman said. "Mine is Nara."

"Carver Reed." I stepped into the clearing around the fire and reached out with my hands, hovered them over the orange glow. I felt the heat, like the clock tower as it burned down.

"Carver Reed," Nara said. "Here is a long way off from anywhere."

"I crossed over in a hotel, in New York," I said. "It brought me over back there, in the middle of the field."

Nara nodded. "There are still some of those. Old places that will let you come to these dead parts of Riven. They are becoming ever scarcer."

"I need to get back to the city," I said. "Can you point me in the right way?"

Now Nara looked up at me, her face bearing traces of wrinkles, her eyes a cloudy blue. You could be whomever you wanted in Riven. You created the image of yourself. Nara eschewed youth for a wiser visage, yet one that bore its age lightly.

"I can," Nara said. "But I have so few visitors. Would you mind staying for a little while and telling me about the world that you came from?"

Nara wasn't a person, I realized. She was a spirit. I should've seen it earlier, recognized the nothing else would bother building a home out here in the wilderness. Only, a spirit that survived long enough to make a place like this one had to be bound by someone else, and the only person I knew binding random spirits was Piotr.

"Who controls you?" I asked. Nara laughed.

"Controls me?" Nara said. "I'm far too old for that."

"You're not bound?"

"What purpose would I serve, way out here?" Nara replied. "Who would find me to bind me in the first place?"

"Your answers are creating more questions."

"I'm afraid that's a habit of mine," Nara said. "So tell me, Carver. Have the Americans won yet?"

"Won?"

"Yes, I believe the last time I saw someone like you, the Americans were fighting for their independence. It was quite the story."

I paused. Nara wasn't talking about the current war, but something over a century past.

"They won," I said, not knowing what else to say.

"Then he would've been disappointed," Nara said, shaking her head. "He spent far too long talking about his great empire. As though he'd forgotten that all empires eventually fall."

"How long have you been here?".

"A long time. When you want very much to stay, Riven doesn't try to move you."

"Spirits can't stay by themselves. Not forever," I said. I realized Nara standing there seemed to contradict that assertion. That the Cycle would always pull a spirit to it eventually. If that wasn't true, then the Cycle was not as strong as I'd been told, or Nara was lying and perhaps Piotr meant for me to come here.

"Have you ever asked yourself how Riven came to be?" Nara said. "Why all of this exists?"

"Only after I've had a few drinks," I replied.

"I've been dry for centuries," Nara said, slipping back to a former time. "The last of the wine vanished long ago."

"What?" I said, because what else was there to say?

"It doesn't matter. You said you wanted to find your way back to the city?" Nara said. I had the impression that she juggled dozens of simultaneous thoughts, leaping from one idea to the next without a clear connection. "Long ago, it actually was one. The city."

"Now it's ruins," I said. "And won't be that for much longer."

"Is it finally falling apart?"

"Too many spirits," I said. "Riven is being overrun."

"Which is why you want to go back?"

I told her everything. I wasn't sure why. Whether it was the soft tones of her voice, the feeling that Nara had infinite amounts of knowledge and equally infinite patience. She did not seem to judge me for my fate or for my part in making Riven what it was. She listened like someone who had no desire to ever talk.

"So I have my reasons," I finished.

"I should say that you do," Nara said. "Except, from what you've said, you lack the skill."

"I have to try."

"If you are victorious, what will you do next?"

"I suppose I'll try to help the guides as best I can. Assuming I'm not locked up forever."

"May I make a suggestion?" Nara asked.

"I feel like you're going to regardless of what I say."

"When you're done, when your quest for vengeance ends, come back here," Nara said. "You say you want to save Riven. I can help you."

"I'm standing here right now? I'll take any hints. Tips."

Nara smiled, a chill pair of lips. A look not flavored with kindness or joy. Rather, she made the gesture seem mechanical. An expected part of conversation and nothing more.

"I've been waiting for a long time," Nara said. "I can wait a little longer. I will help you find your way, and when you are done, you will help me find mine."

Chapter 56
A New Binding

So what do you know about Riven that's going to help me?" I asked Nara as we stood around the fire.

"Such a broad question," Nara replied. "A spirit can learn much in centuries of living here."

"Then, because I don't have centuries, how about we get right to it and you give me the thing that's going to help me the most?"

"Difficult to answer," Nara said. "But if you were to ask me what I could most easily give you, then it would be to tell you about the binding."

"I already know how to do that," I said. Binding a spirit was one of the first things you were taught once you had passed the basic training necessary to become a guide. Bending spirits to your will, if only for a brief time, was integral for searching out breaches, for gaining allies in dangerous situations, or even because you needed someone to talk to. All of that was fine, all of it accepted under guide rules, provided you let the spirit go after you were done. Selena and I chose to ignore that part.

"Then tell me," Nara said. "If you are so sure of yourself, how much of you have you given away?"

"Given away?

"I mean what I say. Have you nurtured those you bound, or do you sustain them? Do you feed them your life to keep them strong or teach them to grow their own?"

Grow their own? Spirits were already dead. They couldn't have their own life. Nara didn't make any sense. But then, here I was talking to a spirit that claimed she lived for centuries in the middle of an endless field of grain. Sense didn't have a large part to play in this particular situation.

"I do what I was taught," I said. "Part of me goes to live with every spirit I bind."

"It doesn't come back?"

"Not unless the binding is broken."

Nara nodded. "That is how it was taught. That is how it was learned. That is not how it has to be."

"You're saying there's another way to bind a spirit?" I said.

"I'm saying that you can get your strength back," Nara said. "While still keeping those you love from going to the Cycle."

"Those I love?"

"Even one as old and alone as I am can tell when a man is talking about one he will not part with," Nara said. "The defensive edge in your tone, the way your eyes find their way to the edge of the clearing. How you needlessly avoid talking about any specific person. It's all how you try to protect the one that you love. I can help you, help her protect you."

"Fine," I said. "Then tell me. Or show me. Or do whatever it is you have to do that's going to give me my strength back. We're wasting time."

I'd felt that boost once before. When the ghoul near the Mountain had broken my binding to Selena and Nicholas. Having that strength back would be a boon against Piotr, an edge I would need to hold my own against him.

"Look for the missing part of you," Nara said. I nodded. "Find it, and find her."

I reached into myself and looked for that small itch, that missing part of me. When I found it, I touched Selena across our bond. Sent a wave of happiness through. She replied in kind. I felt a question come back from her, asking me where I was, what I was doing. I told her only to wait. To listen.

"Now you must withdraw from her," Nara said. "Take it back. Take it all back."

"You mean break the binding?"

Nara shook her head. "Withdraw it. You will see what happens."

Like flexing a muscle, like holding my breath. I took in the connection between Selena and I. Her worry seeped through, the concern she probably felt coming from me. But I didn't stop. Our tie to each other dwindled away except for one tiny sliver, a sliver that I couldn't seem to cut, couldn't seem to close off without severing everything.

"It's almost gone," I said.

"Hold it there," Nara said. "Wait for her. She will learn."

I tried to press reassurance to the tiny bond. Like trying speak through a tiny hole that I could not see. Like trying to find Selena's hand in the dark.

"If she is strong, she will grow her own. To open her own soul and let it thrive," Nara said.

"I don't understand. If she's dead, how can she live without my help?"

"As roots may grow multiple seeds, a proper binding can allow many spirits to flourish without killing the host," Nara said. "What is left within her will grow to fill the space you have provided."

It happened quickly. I kept my focus on my bond to Selena, small and slight though it was. Eventually, like a warm glow from a distant fire, our connection grew. Opened again to a broad and clear path between us. Only this time it was a knot tied with both of us. If before I had focused on myself to find Selena, to reach through our bond, now it was like another sense. Like listening, or hearing. She was a part of me and I a part of her.

My strength came back. Not all of it, but most. As though I'd recovered from an exhausting run.

"That's how he's doing it," I said aloud. "This is how Piotr's binding all of those spirits."

Nara looked at me. "The leader of your guides?"

"He must have figured it out," I said.

"Or had my secrets told to him."

Now it was my turn to glance her way. "Who would have known? You said I was the first one here in a hundred years."

"I'm not the only one capable of passing such knowledge," Nara said, and I felt dumb. Of course. If any one of those guides had known how to bind spirits like this, they could have passed it down from one leader to the next. A secret to keep all of their spirits awake. Waiting for a chance to break out of Riven's chains.

"Thank you," I said. Next I'd have to repeat the process with Nicholas. Grab every bit of myself back that I could.

"Save your thanks," Nara said. "You will give it when you come back."

"I will," I said. "You keep insisting on that, why?"

"Because none of the others have done so." Nara turned back to her fire. "They have taken my knowledge and left me here to rot."

Chapter 57
A Return

Time in Riven was a fluid concept. There weren't days to track, movements of the sun to follow as it trekked across the sky. There was only a growing sense of exhaustion, a tingling awareness that my body back in the real world might need some attention. But there was no going back.

Nara and I even tried, after I insisted. Even if I crossed over into the muzzle of Polk's revolver, I might be able to get some water. A bite to eat. Keep my body from withering.

We followed my trail of flattened and broken stalks to where I crossed over. Under her watchful eyes, I sat down amongst the wheat and tried to cross back. At first, it felt normal. Riven fell away and my soul, or my consciousness, or whatever you want to call it drifted. The feeling of the grain stalks, a pile that we'd made to give me enough of a bed to cross back, fell away.

I floated on water in an endless sea of night. The void that all of us went through while crossing between Riven and our world. After a few seconds I should have woken up on the other side. Instead I kept floating. Something wasn't right.

If you've ever experienced those moments before you fall asleep, those instants where you can tell you're about to slip away into a dream, that's what happened to me. Where my formless, shapeless self started falling into that void.

"They're blocking my way back," Bryce said.

I couldn't wake up. Polk or Derringer, or Piotr, were keeping me asleep. I pulled away from that sweet urge, that surrender to the endless dark. Pushed my soul back to Riven. Focused on the bed of grain, that gray sky, until my eyes opened into Nara's curious face.

"Then you must hurry," Nara said when I explained why I'd come back.

"Any chance you could help with that?" I said. "I don't exactly know my way around here. It all looks the same."

"To an outsider, I suppose it does," Nara said. Then she pointed. "Straight that way. You will catch sight of the city walls before long."

"I will keep my promise," I said to her. "I'll come back for you."

"For me?" Nara said. "No, Carver Reed, I think you will come back for yourself."

Not knowing how to respond to that, I left with a nod. Trudged through the grain until the wall appeared in the distance, its gray bulk shimmering in the view on the horizon and gradually becoming real.

I told Selena I was coming, told her to get Bryce and Alec ready. I had no idea how long Piotr would wait for me. How many days he was willing to lose. Or how much longer I had before Riven fell.

Once I was in the city, though, it was apparent that Riven teetered on the edge. Buildings like the Palace, once dusty but whole, were marred by broken walls and torn gates. Spirits and ghouls taking out their frustration, the telltale gouges of guides striking back with weapons of their own.

I'd asked Nara, asked her if with all the space in the grain fields whether Riven could survive. If the spirits could spread out into the infinite. To which Nara replied that it wasn't about the number of spirits, but their proximity to each other. The collective force that in small amounts can make a ghoul, but in larger ones could form breaches and eventually tear those same holes open.

"Selena said you'd be here," Anna said, stepping out from an alleyway. "I'm not quite believing it. I thought you would be dead for sure."

"I should be," I said. "But Piotr's not ready to give up yet. He doesn't want to risk a wide open gate."

"So instead he sent you east of the city?"

"I don't think he knew where I was going," I said. "Where are you?"

"I'm back with those sneaks in New York. Helping them with client work."

"At least you got away," I said.

"I'm trying to figure out how to rescue you," Anna said as we walked along towards the apartment. "Only it's not easy. Polk and Derringer are in the room all the time, and others usually aren't far away. Piotr himself is gone; I don't know where."

"You could try the police," I said. "Claim I'm being held hostage."

"You might have forgotten," Anna said. "But you're a wanted criminal."

"Hmm, good point. Still, it might be worth it."

"You want me to try? They could prevent you from crossing over."

"Better than being used," I said. "If we can't win, then you have to. You have to get me out of their hands."

Anna nodded. "It's been three days, Carver. Where were you?"

"Lost," I said. "It was really, really boring."

Anna seem to buy the explanation. If she thought I lied, she didn't press me on it. Nobody else needed to know about Nara, for now.

Chapter 58

Armed and Assembled

By the time we made it to the apartment, everyone was already there. Ready and waiting. Bryce held his voulge, wore a new coat that Nicholas had made. Selena had her cleaver. Even Alec returned, shaking his head when I asked him whether he'd found a way to save Bryce.

"He's in lock down," Alec said. "Guides are posted at his house, keeping him in that bed. His family is in a hotel."

"I never thought they would do something like this," Bryce said.

"The punishment is supposed to be terrible to keep other guides from getting ideas."

"Look at how well that's worked for them," Bryce replied.

"All right. After this, Anna, can you work with Alec to break Bryce out?" I asked. "Leverage some of your contacts to get them out of the city?"

"It's like you think I'm some sort of spy master," Anna said.

"Aren't you?"

"I might be able to figure something out," Anna said, shaking her head.

"You would have my gratitude," Bryce said.

"Consider it a thank you for getting me in this mess." Anna twisted her face into a smile. "Without you hiring me, I'd probably have been caught by now. Or maimed by a spirit."

"So what's the plan?" Alec asked. "We head right for the Mountain?"

I nodded. There wasn't much else to it. Carry the fight to Piotr and hope we do better this time than before. Hope that knowing what was coming would be enough. That we could do better than Graham and Katherine.

Nicholas elected to stay back this time. Claimed he'd be better served spending the journey working on other projects. Things he didn't want to get into until he was sure they would work out. I didn't argue. Without the scientist, it'd be one less body to protect.

This time, as we journeyed out, I stayed for the entire hike. The couple of days walking along Riven's avenues, through the wall to the forest and along the same trail traveled by the thousands of spirits going to the Cycle. Alec and Anna crossed in and out as they were able to. Alec took the train by himself, went back to Inman's camp and crime scene. The police had closed the investigation, leaving the cabins deserted. Beds empty and waiting.

As we went, sparks littered the sky. Guides communicating about this or that breach. The howls of spirits, of rage beyond comprehension echoed between the buildings. Riven tearing itself apart in war.

Still, for the first time in days, I had hope.

Chapter 59

Revenge as Planned

The Mountain stood before us, its entrance glowing with the pale blue reflection of the Cycle from deep within. The last time I'd stood there, it'd been with my mother and father. Now, with my mentor and my friend. Selena, the spirit that I loved. With us, a woman I trained; Anna. The sneaks in New York had plenty of beds synced up with various parts of Riven. Including the forest.

Around us the endless march of the dead continued; spirits brushing past on their vacant walk to the Cycle. Behind us, the ghostly trees beckoned with their shivering leaves. I looked at all of my companions and gave them a nod.

"Inside, let me handle Piotr," I said. "Keep the other spirits off of us. If you have to wrangle them, do it. If you don't have to, let them stay. Every bound soul saps a bit of strength from Piotr's swings."

I drew my lash with my right hand, and my left settled on the familiar long knife. Tools made to serve a purpose, to serve an order that no longer wanted me. An order whose leader would see me dead. It felt appropriate that these would be the means of Piotr's end.

We marched into the Mountain, staying in line with Anna at the back, Selena, Bryce, and Alec behind me. We kept going past the offshoots, the tunnels that led to treasures left behind by guides long past. Soon we made it to that central landing, the spot where, before, Piotr's cloak and sword had been. Now, there was nothing.

"Carver," Piotr announced from down the stairs, towards the Cycle. "You've taken your time. I feared you would never show. That your body would simply waste away in that hotel room and you would die a coward."

I couldn't see him, could only hear his echoing voice.

"Piotr, this is between you and me," I called back. "Come out here and let's handle this the way it ought to be."

"A fair fight?" Piotr said. "That's delicious, coming from you. Who tried to ambush me with that girl in New York. No, I think it's best you earn your audience."

"Behind!" Anna yelled, and we turned. A group of former guides, sporting all manner of weapons and cloaks, broke through the line of dead spirits. They slid through the spirit crowd, dancing between the dead without pausing. Without getting tripped up by the many feet or pushed aside by apathetic shoulders.

I had to remind myself that these were not normal foes, but the best the guides had to offer. Leaders bound to serve the next one in this endless chain until, with the gateway or with the end of my lash, the chain could be broken.

"Go Carver," Selena said. "We can hold them."

Bryce push me towards the stairs as he drew his voulge. "Don't let this be for nothing."

My mentor, always inspiring. I took off down the steps as the clash of metal rang out behind me. My friends fighting for their lives.

About time I fought for mine.

At the bottom of the stairs the cave widened out into the flat landing before the great blue ocean of the Cycle. Piotr stood near the edge, watching spirits step off into oblivion. Facing me, though, were two spirits that I thought I'd lost.

"Hello Carver," Graham said, his hammer sitting on his shoulder.

"About time you showed up," Katherine said to me, my mother idly tossing one of her batons up and down. "We were getting bored waiting for you."

"Isn't it a pleasant surprise, Carver?" Piotr said. "Your parents. Still alive, such as it is. Think about it; you could return them home. Just lie down and give yourself up."

There's a certain type of anger that takes you over. That leaves you breathless and focused. That obliterates all consideration of anything other than the source. That renders reality into a single white hot dot and you can't think about anything else. Can't do anything except lash out against it in a ceaseless frenzy. Piotr was that dot, and I would erase him.

I took a step towards Piotr and my parents closed the gap. Graham raised his wrist, that same contraption ready to fire one of its burning wires. I swung with the lash, cracked it against Graham's gadget. The lash's coil wrapped around the metal and I pulled back so hard that the gadget itself tore off of Graham's wrist and flew back towards me.

I snapped the lash, still coiled around the gadget. Aimed it at Katherine, coming in at me from my right side. She swept her baton up through the gadget, hooking it and pulling hard. Trying to tear the lash from my grasp. Only I wasn't the same guide that I had been. For one, with Nara's trick, I'd grown stronger. For two, I had no concerns.

No hesitation.

No fear.

Piotr had brought me to the edge of reason. To the point where there was nothing left except this fight, this victory. So I twisted my shoulder and pulled. Swept my arm and dragged my mother and her baton with it. Knocked her into Graham as he stepped forward with the hammer. They fell over each other to the ground.

I didn't hesitate. Ran up, and used the knife. First my mother, and then my father. Two stabs, two blue fire burns, and my parents were gone. Again.

"Impressive," Piotr said. "Though I suppose I shouldn't be surprised. They didn't want to hurt you. They resisted so heavily."

"Resisted?" I looked into their blank eyes as my parents rose up.

"Have you ever seen Graham open with that wrist of his?" Piotr said, drawing his great sword and leveling out towards me. "Why would Katherine try to catch your lash instead of simply dodging, cutting underneath and delivering her strikes? Your parents let you win."

I reached my hand towards my mother. There was a chance, now that they had been separated from Piotr, that I could rebind them. Perhaps make this a three on one. Then I saw Piotr's sword shift in the corner my eye. Whistle towards me in a long cut the forced me back from my parents.

"Time for these two to have peace, don't you think?" Piotr said. My parents, oblivious to the world, turned and walked those fateful steps to the Cycle. Only moments until they fell.

"I think you need to stop talking," I said, raising the lash. Piotr shuffled back from my first strike, the lash falling short. Moved himself away from my parents and I, towards the left edge.

I followed, using the lash to keep Piotr and his waving great sword at a distance. Every time it cracked, I forced him back another inch. Closer and closer to that ever-present blue. I spared a glance as my parents walked out on that short precipice with the other spirits. About to leap into the Cycle.

I wouldn't be able to get to them. I wasn't sure I wanted to. They deserved their rest. They had suffered enough. If I wanted to pay back their memory, I would do it by sending Piotr along with them.

Chapter 60

Up Close and Cutting

My lash's shadow shot a curling line through the Cycle's glow as it reflected on the cavern walls. My knife partnered with it, a straight edge pointing up towards Piotr's throat. He stayed out of range, across the room. The crowd of wandering spirits divided us as they marched endlessly into the blue lake. Piotr's great sword towered above them.

"I can say that this is refreshing," Piotr said. "To finally meet someone worthy. A test after all these years."

"I'm not a test," I said. "This isn't a game."

"Then prove it to me."

The large man shifted forward, elbowing his way into the line of spirits and through the other side. Right into my lash's cracking strike.

The lash hit him in the shoulder, the point digging into Piotr's skin. Boring a hole through his coat. But Piotr was too broad for the lash to wrap around. He shrugged off the attack, continuing his advance. Piotr lowered his shoulder and leaned forward, bringing the great sword in a cleaving swing that would've split me in two. If I'd stayed put.

I darted back, putting distance between us. The great sword missed my face by a foot, the black and silver blade flashing reflected light as it went past. Plenty of room for my lash to strike again. I snared Piotr's right arm as his swing carried it into the lash's path. The cord curled around Piotr's forearm and held fast. I tightened my grip, held the lash out wide to keep Piotr from moving the sword back into position.

For his part, the leader of the guides stared at my lash around his wrist, as though he couldn't believe he'd actually been tagged.

"The problem with upstarts like you," Piotr said. "Is that they don't understand their history."

"History?" I dashed forward with the knife. One strong stab and maybe I could force Piotr over the edge. Into the Cycle, from where there was no return.

"Every leader that came before has trained me," Piotr said as I went for the stab. "Every tactic discovered through the years, through centuries, I have learned."

As my knife neared his chest, Piotr dropped the sword and swung his hand, the one bound with the lash, into my strike. My own knife cut into the cord and severed it as the great sword hit the ground. I kept my stab going, pushed forward as the blade pierced Piotr's coat, cut into his chest.

I felt his big hands on my arm, pushing the knife back and away. His knee shot up into my stomach, and Piotr threw me to the ground. The man's strength was incredible. I had no way to counter that. I felt light and loose in his grasp, like a thread in the wind.

Piotr grabbed his sword as I pulled up to my feet. I was down a lash, and my knife looked awfully small next to that great sword. I'd have to change tactics.

"But with all the benefits come the costs," Piotr said turning towards me. Raising his weapon. "I know everything, Carver. All of Riven's secrets."

"You think so?"

"I know this place is doomed," Piotr said. "The only hope we have lies in finding a way out."

Piotr slashed the sword towards me, but it was lazy. Forced me back, but not fast enough to go for a kill. My hands felt the back wall of the room, the smooth rock carved out by whatever ancient engineer put this cave together.

"You're not dead," I said. "You don't need to stay here."

"We all come to Riven eventually," Piotr said following my retreat. "I'm choosing to plan in advance."

As Piotr stepped into another swing, I broke into a run. This time towards the line of spirits. They provided some cover, gave me a chance to think. I shoved my way through a pair of nurses, both bearing the scars of disease. Behind me, I heard Piotr's sword bite into the same spirits. Carving and twisting them away. Clearing a path by murdering the dead.

"Stop running, Carver," Piotr said. "I have other things I'd like to do."

"Sorry," I said, and as Piotr broke through the line of spirits, I drew and fired Inman's gun. Still had it, still had bullets even after all this time. Piotr didn't see it coming, only managed to widen his eyes in shock as the bullet bit into his chest.

I followed up the strike, throwing the knife ahead of me and, as Piotr moved to block it, grabbing his hands and fighting for his sword. Piotr might be stronger than me but I hoped that, with surprise on my side, I could wrest the weapon away.

I went for dirty tricks. Kneed Piotr in the stomach, jammed my heel into his foot, and dug my fingernails into his hands as we wrestled for the sword. It wasn't enough. For the first time, I heard Piotr growl, a gravelly aching rumble of pain, and he used his shoulders to clear me away.

"Unexpected," Piotr said. "I should have figured you would use that coward's weapon. It suits you."

Piotr leaned into another swing, and I did the only thing I could think of. I grabbed a spirit walking by on my left and threw him into the path of the blade. Piotr's attack bit into the spirit, but the ghost stopped the sword's momentum. Gave me an opening. I ran up and stuck my right foot behind Piotr's right ankle, pressed against the man's shoulders as he tried to free the sword from the spirit. Sent Piotr toppling to the ground.

Piotr's hands fell free of the sword as I tripped him, and I turned to grab his weapon. Pulled it the rest of the way out of the spirit, who stared at the wound without comprehension. Who turned and continued his walk. Who leapt into the Cycle without knowing that his miserable existence punctuated the end of a tyrant.

I stood over Piotr with his great sword held in my hands.

"Tell me one more time," I said, "about all that knowledge."

Chapter 61

Last Look

I saw the anger, the fury and fear drain out of Piotr's face in that moment. The man I'd once regarded as a wise sage, a leader in times of darkness, now simply looked like an old man.

"You've won," Piotr said. "I admit it; I'm done. Your victory is yours and, with it, a chance to see the ruin of this world."

"Looking forward to it," I said, raising the sword.

"There is something you should see," Piotr said. "Normally, when a guide leader falls, the transition is more orderly. The spirit has time to convey the information. To tell their replacement what they need to know."

"Already got that, thanks," I said, thinking of Nara, but I hesitated. Piotr might be telling the truth. Who knew what kind of secrets he had, or tools he knew about that might help after I sent him to the Cycle.

"Not everything. Let me stand. Keep the sword. Press it against my back for all I care."

"Where?"

"It's not far. As evil as you think I am, Carver, I truly don't wish to see everything collapse to ashes. I did want to save Riven."

Part of me wanted to deliver the deathblow right then and there. Burn Piotr with wrangling fire and send him into the Cycle. But what if I would be throwing away the one thing that could help us restore Riven? To drive back the spirits and keep us safe? Didn't I have a responsibility?

"Go on then," I said. "If I see anything, if I see those hands move, I'll strike before you get anywhere."

"I would expect nothing less," Piotr replied, and then I let him stand. Let him lead me out of the chamber and back up the stairs towards the landing. Except, halfway up, he turned to the right and went through a small passage. One I'd skipped over, assuming it, like all the others, led to the lost bed of an old guide.

Instead the path wound steadily up, curling in on itself. Narrow steps carved into the rock led us through a darkened passage as the Cycle's blue glow dimmed. Soon a familiar gray light replaced it. Outside.

"Where are we going?" I asked.

"The guides used to live in the Mountain," Piotr said. "Hundreds of years before I was born the guides operated out of these caves. Only when the spirits began to cross over into the city did we move our operation. Over time, there was less and less need to come here. Less need to know where the spirits went after we took away their anger."

"That doesn't answer my question."

"So you understand," Piotr said. "We're going to where the guides kept watch. To where they could see spirits amassing, could see the ghouls do their work. Could plan their nightly raids."

A few moments later I saw that Piotr wasn't lying. The passageway opened onto a rocky slope, high above the door where we'd come in. The dark forest spread out beneath us and in the distance I could make out Riven's city; its wall a dark line on the horizon. Beneath us the crowded trail of spirits marched towards the Mountain from miles away.

"From here, a watcher could see a signal from anywhere. From the city walls, even, a guide could launch a spark when they were in trouble and expect aid to come."

"Why did we come here?" I said. "This won't help us."

Climbing the steps, making my way to the narrow passage, I hadn't been able to keep the great sword at the ready. I hadn't held it to Piotr's throat since we stepped up on the slopes. Had kept it gripped in my hands, but not in a position to strike. So I did nothing when Piotr pulled a sparker from his belt and held it up into the air.

"No," Piotr said. "But it will help me."

Piotr pressed the button on the bottom of the sparker and glimmering golden yellow motes launched high in the air, flaring bright against the ashen sky.

"What was that?" I said, bringing Piotr's sword to rest against his throat.

"The last signal I need to send," Piotr said.

"To who?"

Piotr only laughed.

I fell away. That's the only way I can think of to describe it. Me, the physical me, stood still on that slope with Piotr's great sword held against his throat. My spirit, my soul, shivered. Dropped as though I had fallen down an unending well.

Parts of me split away as I plummeted. First, with a tearing rend like scraping my knee on concrete, went the bonds I'd formed with Selena and Nicholas. Wrenched away and gone.

Next fled the tingling sensation, the warning my spirit had been giving me for days now that I needed to cross back. That didn't tear away. It vanished, as though the feeling had never been there at all.

I still fell, still rushed through oblivion as every part of me split and came back together, bent and turned and twisted. As though I was severely ill and, at the same time, crashing into the earth.

I blinked.

Piotr stared at me along the length of his blade. His eyes were questioning, curious.

"How does it feel?" Piotr asked.

I glanced down at myself. Everything appeared to be there. I could feel my fingers gripping the hilt of the sword, could feel Riven's chilled breeze on my body. Could feel my lungs attempting to breathe Riven's non-air. And yet . . .

"What did you do?"

"Carver," Piotr replied. "You're dead."

Chapter 62

New Life

I didn't have a rational way of dealing with the words. I hadn't prepared for this. No scenario I'd plotted had this as a possibility. With my parents, Bryce and I had spent part of the journey over here talking about how they might show up.

I'd expected Piotr to try and persuade me to give up my life. One more opportunity to take the easy way out.

I'd planned to deal with a fight that I might lose, and had kept Inman's pistol as a surprise.

Bryce and I had practiced the grappling, him holding his voulge like a sword so that I'd know how to wrest it from Piotr's grasp.

If I was going to die, we all assumed it would be by Piotr's hand. Instead, it had been Derringer's gun, or a knife in a hotel room in New York. My body hadn't fought to survive. I'd been murdered.

"You gave up," I said. I searched, inside, for that connection. That tie to my physical self, but there was nothing. "You'll never open your gate."

"Does it matter?" Piotr said, nodding out over the expanse of Riven in front of us. "Look at it. All of those points, those pools of light?"

I followed his eyes. Speckled like stars on the night sky were shimmering circles, the closer ones in the forest revealing themselves as Piotr called them. Pools.

"They're breaches," Piotr continued. "Every single one of them. More appear every hour. Riven is overrun. I'll either escape when one of those angry spirits tears a hole, or I'll be too dead to care."

"It'll be the latter," I said. I pulled the blade back and, with a single clean stroke, ended Piotr's reign as the leader of the guides.

His body crumpled to the ground, then rose. A pure spirit now. One that could live again. Except I was waiting. Twisted the hilt on the great sword and burned out the glimmer of a soul in Piotr's eyes.

He left me there on the slope, walked back into the tunnel on the path to the Cycle.

I don't know how long I stood there, watching the breaches glow on the sprawling landscape beneath me. There weren't guides operating in the forest. Spirits crossing from those breaches would continue to pour out, find each other, and feed off of their anger to become ghouls or packs of roving, maiming monsters.

Piotr was gone. The Master, as we'd called him during those months trying to find out who he was, had met his end. Riven, though, seemed as bad as it had been before.

"Carver?" Selena's voice came up out of the Mountain, carrying up the passageway.

"Up here," I replied and before long Selena joined me on the mountainside. "Is everyone all right?"

Selena took in the view, then settled on the ground next to me. She spared a long look for Piotr's great sword. "We're still here, if that counts. Alec took some scrapes, so he and Anna are crossing back over."

"Good," I said. "They'll need their energy. And Bryce?"

"He's waiting for us back near the Cycle. Watching to make sure all the spirits Piotr bound go in."

"Always about the mission with him."

"I saw Piotr go over the edge," Selena said. "That means it's over, right?"

"One part," I said. "Tell me, can you feel it?"

"Feel what?"

"The binding. You and I."

I watched her eyes as they closed briefly, as Selena searched for the tie that had kept us together for more than a year. Watched as she opened them, took her hand, and placed it over mine.

"I can teach you," Selena said. "How to resist the Cycle. It will get easier."

"And this?" I waved my hand at the view. "I don't know how to deal with that. There's no way we can face all of those breaches."

"Maybe not," Selena said. "But we've gone up against some terrible monsters before and come out alive. So to speak, anyway."

We stayed there on the slope for a while longer, counting the breaches and measuring our affection in the silence. For our entire relationship, Selena had been dependent on my binding to keep her away from the Cycle. Now, for the first time, I would need her help, her support, to resist it. To guide me.

Chapter 63

Hold the Thread

The whispers started on what Bryce said was the second day. We were in the forest, the three of us walking by spirits marching the other way, when I heard them. Soft and indistinct, like the remnants of a dream upon waking up. Less real words than urges. A pull to turn back, to return to the Cycle.

"Laugh," Selena said when she noticed I'd stopped, when she and Bryce made it a few paces ahead. "Think of something funny."

"That's hard to do on command," I said. But I did. Reached and replayed a memory of one of the many times Nicholas had detonated himself in his lab, all in the interest of research. A ruined oven and a scientist with his hair on fire, his coat charred and missing patches.

The whispers stopped with my smile. Faded away, though I could still feel it. Like the tiniest thirst, lingering at the edge of my senses.

"It worked," I said, and Selena nodded. Bryce, I noticed, kept his eyes on me a little longer. One of his hands had gone behind his back, ready to draw his voulge.

I was a spirit, unbound and capable of turning at any moment. I'd have done the same thing in Bryce's place.

Selena continued dropping tips as we made our way back to the city. Tricks like laughing, or focusing on a treasured memory. Or a loved one. Anything that brought you into your own humanity. That's what kept the Cycle at bay.

"It never truly goes away, does it?" I asked her as we went through the western gate to the city.

"You get used to it," Selena said. "After a while it's like anything else. Something you deal with."

As if coping with death wasn't enough.

Alec met us back at the apartment with a burst of good news. He'd been communicating with other guide leaders and, after pondering the situation, they'd decided to give Bryce his life back.

"And more than that," Alec said. "Since you're the ranking guide, Bryce, we're going to vote to make you the new leader."

"I don't want it," Bryce said. "I'm retired."

"Don't think you have a choice," Alec replied. "You saw all of those breaches. If we're going to have a chance, we need someone that can bring the guides together. It's not going to be me."

Bryce glowered in Alec's direction.

"Bryce," I said. "Take it. You'd be the best leader the guides have ever seen. You know Riven inside and out, already have connections on the other side, and with me over here, you've got your spirit emissary all figured out."

"Spirit emissary?" Bryce asked.

"I figured you'd want to create a new position," I replied. "Someone that helps connect you with the spirits that aren't angry, that don't want to cross over quite yet."

"You're all assuming Riven's going to be around much longer," Bryce said. "You're trying to make me the captain of a sinking ship."

"Because you're the only one that can save her."

Bryce grumbled for a little while longer, but he didn't have any more fight left in him. By the time he left to cross back with Alec, the two were already talking allocations and adjustments, what regions needed more support, and how they could drive recruitment.

I watched them head towards the clock tower, a pair that I'd once made a trio, and felt lost.

"I see you picked up a new weapon?" Nicholas asked, kneeling behind me to inspect Piotr's great sword. I'd carried it back from the Mountain, as with the lash severed I needed some sort of defense.

"It's a trophy," I replied.

"Rather deadly for a trophy," Nicholas said. "The carvings on this are exquisite. I'd say it goes back at least a hundred years or more. Possibly ancient. Some of it, anyway."

"Some of it?"

"Yes. It looks like your sword is a composite. I can pick out at least three different types of iron and steel. Points at which they've been joined. If this were out on the other side, such a technique would make a weapon like this prone to shattering," Nicholas shifted his goggles up above his eyes. "In Riven? Perhaps it works differently."

I hefted the sword and looked at it, the black and silver streaks running down the blade. The runes I couldn't read appearing every couple of inches on the metal. The hilt, a curling gold and green design that bled into a bronzed guard. Piotr never explained where he'd found it. With him gone, the sword's origin would remain an unknown story.

Maybe I would use it to tell a new one.

Chapter 64

Overrun

"You say we have to go back?" Selena said. "Away from the breaches that we could be closing?"

"I made a promise," I said as we packed up our weapons. The crossbow hung over my back, the great sword hanging beneath it. My knife and lash, newly repaired by Nicholas, hung on my waist. Food and drink weren't necessary. They never would be.

"To who, again?"

"An old spirit. Goes by the name of Nara, though I'm not sure that's what she's really called," I said. "She says she can help."

"I thought you said spirits couldn't stay in Riven unless they were bound?"

"I did," I said. "Either I'm wrong, or someone's controlling her. I'm hoping for the former."

Nara hadn't said what she wanted me to do, why she wanted me to come back, but if she'd managed to survive unbound in Riven for hundreds of years, then I wanted to know her secret. I wanted to know how to stay.

Anna and Alec would be arriving soon, to help take us to the city's eastern gates. I went out to the balcony, Selena's favorite viewing spot, and watched the sparks explode over Riven's broken buildings. Cries echoed down the alleys as ash swirled through the sky. A city of the dead full of life.

This was my home now, and I would fight for it.

Read on for an excerpt from SPIRIT'S END - the finale to The Riven Trilogy!

An Excerpt from SPIRIT'S END

The Riven Trilogy Book Three

I had been alive the last time I kissed her lips. Soft, cool to the touch. Mine were likely the same. Selena's eyes, though, still had life. Her soul was still there. Mine too.

We parted, grabbed our things from around the gray, ashy apartment. I slipped on my long black coat, a reminder of something I no longer was. A guide, meant to take the spirits of Earth's dead stuck in Riven and send them on. Send them to the Cycle to keep them from crowding out this world. This grand, desolate place.

My home.

I hooked my lash into my belt, a ten foot long cord with a piercing metal point at the end. On my left side, I stuck in a long knife, a foot and a half of pointed desperation. On my back went the great sword I'd taken from the man who killed me. The sword stood half my height and took both hands to swing. Its black and silver metal blade would have been heavy, but without a real body and its limitations, I had no problems hefting the weapon. I didn't get tired anymore.

My crossbow hung over the sword, three sets of bolts looping around the shaft. Normal black-tipped quarrels meant to deliver pointed pain to anything they struck. Next were blue ones, ready to spit out wrangling fire that would deliver a spirit to its peaceful end. Last came orange. A shot that could be as dangerous to me as it was to the enemy. My favorite.

"You're sure this is what we should do?" Selena said as she set her cleaver, as long as a knife and as thick as my sword, with biting ridges on the front edge, in its holster attached to the front flap of her coat.

"I don't know," I said. "But if Nara doesn't have an idea, we're stuck. Breaches are erupting everywhere, and the guides don't have the numbers. We need a miracle, and unless you've thought one up in the last couple of hours, that spirit is our best shot."

I didn't bring up the other reason for speed. The voice whispering at the edge of my mind, calling me to drop everything I had and start on that long walk to oblivion. The Cycle murmured, always there. A honeyed hush inviting me to give up my troubles and embrace peace.

And they said the dead had no worries.

"Is it strong today?" Selena noticed my closed eyes. "Bad?"

She asked me every morning. Her passion kept the Cycle in check. If I focused on her, on what Selena was saying, what we had, then the Cycle's siren call would diminish. Selena gave me a reason to stay, one far more compelling than the Cycle's push to leave.

"No worse than any other." I ran my hand over my face, gave her a slapdash smile.

Selena gave me a hard stare for a moment. She knew when I wasn't telling her the whole truth. I didn't have time for that discussion now, though. Bigger things to worry about.

"You ready?" I moved to the door. "Alec and Anna should be coming soon."

"You're the one with a dozen weapons." Selena didn't need blades to be deadly, though the two she carried were enough. One harsh look from those icy eyes and any spirit ought to run away.

Find SPIRIT'S END at your favorite bookstore!

Acknowledgments

There's this idea that writing is a solitary act, but that couldn't be further from the truth. Every writer depends on friends, family, and, yes, the readers to keep spinning their stories.

Specifically, I'd like to thank my wife, Nicole, who's endless love and encouragement make every day brighter. My brothers, Jonathan, Justin, and Matthew, and parents, Bob and Mary, who help keep a smile on my face.

And, of course, all of you readers that make this life possible.

Thank you.

About the Author

A.R. Knight writes sci-fi and fantasy in the frozen north of Wisconsin. With a pair of cats keeping him company, he enjoys delving into adventures that are as much about the villain as the hero.

After getting a degree in journalism and touring the country installing healthcare software, A.R. Knight thought it would be good to get back to what he loved. So now he's got a small office and early mornings to spin whatever tales come into his imagination.

When he's not writing, A.R. Knight tends to travel anywhere he can, whether that's islands off the coast of Ecuador, the rainforest, snowboarding in the Rocky Mountains, or sipping scotch in Edinburgh. That's the nice thing about the writing life, you can take it anywhere.

To contact or see what he's up to, visit www.adamrknight.com

For Justin